The bedroom door burst open without warning.

Jake sat up fast, hand on his weapon. "What's wrong?" he asked quickly, searching over her shoulder for threats.

She marched over to him like a little girl playing soldier. "This is what's wrong."

She reached down, grabbed him by both shoulders and kissed him. Not a how-do-you-do kiss. A wet, open-mouthed, tongue-down-his-throat, I-want-to-do-naughty-things-to-you-right-now sort of kiss.

What the—

"Shannon!" he mumbled against her mouth.

"Shut up and kiss me."

Dear Reader,

Finally the long wait is over. Howdy's book has arrived! When I originally wrote the CHARLIE SQUAD series, I always intended for the team's sniper to have a book of his own. But due to circumstances beyond everyone's control, the series stopped after five books and he was left hanging.

I am so grateful to my marvelous editor, Patience Smith, for her enthusiasm when I (extremely hesitantly) brought up the idea of revisiting CHARLIE SQUAD and giving Howdy his own book at last. My warmest thanks also to all of the readers who have written me to ask for Howdy's story. Without you, this book never would have happened.

Five years have passed for you, my patient reader, and five years have also passed for Charlie Squad and Jake "Howdy" Harrington. Their story picks up where it left off and the adventure continues. I invite you now to join Jake as his story finally comes full circle.

Happy reading!

Cindy Dees

CINDY DEES

The Longest Night

ROMANTIC *SUSPENSE*

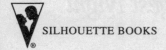

SILHOUETTE BOOKS

Recycling programs
for this product may
not exist in your area.

ISBN-13: 978-0-373-27687-5

THE LONGEST NIGHT

Copyright © 2010 by Cynthia Dees

Visit Silhouette Books at www.eHarlequin.com

Printed in U.S.A.

CINDY DEES

started flying airplanes while sitting in her dad's lap at the age of three and got a pilot's license before she got a driver's license. At age fifteen, she dropped out of high school and left the horse farm in Michigan where she grew up to attend the University of Michigan.

After earning a degree in Russian and East European Studies, she joined the U.S. Air Force and became the youngest female pilot in its history. She flew supersonic jets, VIP airlift and the C-5 Galaxy, the world's largest airplane. She also worked part-time gathering intelligence. During her military career, she traveled to forty countries on five continents, was detained by the KGB and East German secret police, got shot at, flew in the first Gulf War, met her husband and amassed a lifetime's worth of war stories.

Her hobbies include professional Middle Eastern dancing, Japanese gardening and medieval reenacting. She started writing on a one-dollar bet with her mother and was thrilled to win that bet with the publication of her first book in 2001. She loves to hear from readers and can be contacted at www.cindydees.com.

This book is dedicated to all the people who made it happen—the readers who persisted in asking when Howdy was finally going to get his own book, and its editors, Patience Smith and Shana Smith, without whom this project would neither have happened nor lived up to its potential. All of you rock!

Chapter 1

Jake Harrington whistled low under his breath as he stepped into the cavernous black space lit mostly by the glow of the many computer monitors lining the football field–size floor. There were caves, and then there were *caves*.

"Welcome to H.O.T. Watch Ops, Major Harrington," a familiar voice said from nearby.

Jake looked up sharply. Brady Hathaway. A hell of a soldier. Hell of a man. They shook hands and clapped each other on the shoulders.

"How've you been, Howdy?" Hathaway asked warmly.

Jake let a rare hint of a smile light his eyes for his former comrade-in-arms. "I'm good. You're looking…tan."

"It's a real hardship tour living on a gorgeous Caribbean island like this, but someone's gotta do it. What've you been up to? Still too strong and silent to succumb to a woman?"

Jake threw him a withering look. In his line of work a *social* life was impossible, let alone a love life. It wasn't that he didn't crave being a normal guy from time to time. He'd love to meet a woman and pursue a real relationship. But it just wasn't possible.

Hathaway laughed. "It's good to see you haven't changed a bit, Mr. Grinch."

Jake was used to being accused of having no sense of humor. Hell, they usually accused him of having no personality. Thing was, he couldn't imagine running around being Mr. Chatty Cheerful while he killed people for a living. It seemed… disrespectful.

Besides, his work required him to exercise reserves of discipline that most people couldn't even fathom. It wasn't uncommon for him to lie still in the same place for three days at a time. And by still, he meant not a twitch. Not to scratch his nose, not to eat, not to stretch out a cramp. He barely blinked in such hides. Over the years, that capacity for utter physical stillness had translated into a capacity for utter emotional stillness, as well.

His life was a glassy smooth lake. Unruffled. Serene. Yeah, and bland, boring and lonely. But a guy had to take the bad with the good.

Hathaway led him into the middle of the cave through rows of computer terminals and analysts. It looked like a NASA control room. Hathaway stopped in front of a man working at three flat-screen monitors each the size of his television at home and said, "Jake, this is Carter Baigneaux. His handle's Boudreaux or just Boo. Carter, this is Jake Harrington, the sniper I told you about. Field handle Howdy."

The man at the console nodded at Jake and pulled several thick manila folders that looked stuffed with mostly photographs out of a file drawer at his knee.

Hathaway continued, "Carter's a Special Forces man, himself. He spotted what we're about to show you."

Jake frowned. Then why did they need him to look at whatever it was?

Hathaway picked up a slim red folder. "Take a look at this."

Jake opened the file and picked up the top photograph inside. It was a grainy close-up of a man. A man he knew all too well. But why he'd been brought all the way out to this supersecret island to look at a picture of a dead man mystified him. He thumbed through the rest of the pictures, all of them surveillance photos of the same individual.

He glanced up at Hathaway, frowning. "That's Eduardo Ferrare, a drug lord my teammates and I tracked down and killed about five years back. Where'd you get these? I thought I'd seen every photo in existence of the guy, but I don't remember these shots."

Hathaway and Baigneaux exchanged significant looks with each other, and the atmosphere around the two men abruptly crackled with tension.

"What's going on?" Jake bit out, dropping the file onto Carter's desk.

Hathaway said heavily, "I'd better start at the beginning." He gestured at a pair of empty chairs beside Carter, and Jake sank into one. He stretched out his legs to ease a sharp pain in his bum knee and crossed his arms. Once comfortable, he settled into his usual statuelike stillness.

Hathaway gestured around him. "This facility was built to allow us to do high-grade surveillance and monitoring of the Caribbean, and Central and South America. From here, we can see a gnat on a goat anywhere in this part of the world."

Carter grinned and corrected, "We can see the gnat's naughty bits."

Jake sent a mild but quelling glance over at the Cajun. The guy subsided, muttering good-naturedly about seeing what Hathaway meant when he said Harrington was no fun.

Hathaway continued. "Carter picked up some interesting traffic patterns around a house in St. George, Gavarone, a few months ago. He ID'd several known drug dealers going in and out of the place. Not street punks, mind you. Players."

Jake nodded. Men like Eduardo Ferrare had been before Charlie Squad blew him up and burned his body almost past recognition.

"Carter started a photo dossier and inventoried all the visitors to the place over a two month period. He got images of about twenty targets from a high-resolution satellite camera, and commenced identifying them. Boo, here, happens to have developed some of the top face recognition software in the business. It was all going along swimmingly until he ran into one guy. When the face-recognition program popped up the ID, we knew there had to be an error."

When Hathaway quit talking and showed no inclination to continue, Jake sighed and reluctantly took the bait. "And you knew it was an error because?"

"Because the guy in the picture is dead."

A low-level hum of disquiet started in his gut. He had an inkling where this was going, and it was *impossible*. When Charlie Squad killed someone, the target didn't get back up. Ever. They confirmed *all* of their kills.

Jake leaned forward. "Are you telling me you think Ferrare is still alive?"

"You tell me. You just ID'd the guy off a picture taken three weeks ago."

It took every ounce of his self-discipline not to leap up out of his chair. No *way* was Eduardo Ferrare still alive! Fury jostled with dismay in his gut, but disbelief ultimately beat them both out.

"We pulled up the dossier on Ferrare," Hathaway continued, "and saw that Charlie Squad ran a surveillance and infiltration mission on him a while back. Since you were the team's sniper and most likely to have studied the photos in the greatest detail, we wanted to show you Carter's pictures to see what you made of them." He picked up the file and held it out to Jake again. "Take another look. Tell me if you can say that this *isn't* Eduardo Ferrare."

Frowning, Jake took the folder. He flipped it open. Studied the first picture intently. It showed a white stucco portico with a black Mercedes parked in front of it. The car sat low and heavy. Armored, he noted absently. A big guy stood in front of it, his back to the vehicle, in a classic bodyguard pose. Behind the vehicle was a similar guy. Beside the rear passenger door stood three men in a cluster. Two had their backs to the camera, but the third one's face was clearly visible from this angle.

A face he knew as well as his own. A face he'd studied for hundreds of hours, both in pictures and through the sights of his sniper rifle. From every conceivable angle, displaying every conceivable expression.

He breathed, "Sonofa—"

Hathaway said dryly, "I gather you stand by your initial identification, then?"

Jake looked up, grim. "Yeah. That's Eduardo Ferrare. But—" He broke off. It took a hell of a lot to shock him, but he was nigh unto speechless right now.

Hathaway finished for him. "—but Ferrare definitely died in Gavarone five years ago." He and his teammates had been in the tiny South American country monitoring the lead-up to a civil war there and had crossed paths with the drug lord then. They almost hadn't made it out alive.

"I watched the guy's house blow up around him. Hell, he died in Joe Rodriguez's arms. We had the guy's *body*. The clothes, the jewelry, the dental records… We had a *positive* ID. Eduardo Ferrare is *dead*."

Hathaway spoke quietly. "Then who in the hell is the man in that picture?"

Jake stared down at the damning photograph. For all the world, he'd swear that was Eduardo Ferrare...if he didn't know better. "Have you got any pics of the guy's right hand?"

Carter frowned. "Why?"

"He had a pinkie ring he always wore. Unusual kite-shaped diamond. Big rock. Flashy. Except..."

While Carter fished through the stack of pictures, Hathaway asked quietly, "Except what?"

"We got the ring, too. He was wearing it when he died. Our forensics guys matched it to the insurance spectrographs of the stone. It was Ferrare's ring we took off the corpse."

Carter pulled out a picture. "This picture has a good view of his right hand. I can digitally enhance it and see if there's a ring."

Jake watched as the guy turned to his computer and called up a digital file of the picture in question. Carter highlighted a small section of the photograph, the bit that included a fuzzy image of the Ferrare look-alike's hands, and typed in a rapid set of commands.

Carter pulled a microphone down from the side of his head, where he'd folded it back along his narrow headset. "Anyone running a red-priority operation on Big Bertha?" Carter's question resonated over a loudspeaker throughout the cave. Several seconds of silence greeted the announcement.

"Big Bertha?" Jake echoed.

Hathaway murmured, "Our supercomputer array."

"No cleanups in progress on Aisle Four," Jake muttered.

Hathaway grinned, then said, "Have at it, Boo."

Carter typed in a final set of commands. His computer screen went black, replaced by a slowly spinning hourglass.

In a rare fit of something unidentifiable, Jake asked, "How long is this going to take?" Was this actually impatience? He filed the novel sensation as interesting and released a long, slow breath. Calm suffused him. Better.

Carter answered, "Should be no more than a minute or so. I only asked Bertha to enhance a tiny piece of the picture."

Sometimes he felt like a dinosaur, working with his single-shot, manual-loading, Barrett fifty-caliber sniper rifle. The technology had been around for about fifty years now. Oh, sure, his telescopic sights were the latest and greatest technology to be had. He routinely made positive ID's on targets at a range of two miles, and killed them with impunity from well over a mile.

But the things this roomful of computers could do were frankly mind-boggling. Like the picture slowly forming on the screen before him. It had been taken from one-hundred eighty miles above the earth's surface. In a few seconds, he'd be able to see if the guy in the picture was wearing a ring... and if so, what kind.

"Here it comes," Carter murmured.

Pixels started to fill the screen rapidly. A Mercedes hood ornament came into view, and the torso of a man behind it. A forearm, and then a hand, began to take shape.

Jake leaned forward. Was that a ring forming? Surely not. And *surely* not a kite-shaped diamond that winked like a star when light hit it just right.

A bright spot of white appeared at the edge of the man's hand. A vague stripe crossed his pinkie finger.

No.

But no matter how much he wished it not to be so, Jake knew the ring taking shape on the man's hand. The image finished loading, and the three men stared at the kite-shaped diamond sparkling back at them.

Hathaway commented from behind him, "Looks like we've got us a match, boys."

Jake frowned. "Is there any way we can find out if the ring's still in government custody?"

Baigneaux commented, "I can run that down...but jewelry can be duplicated."

Jake frowned. "For that matter, a face can be duplicated. But why would somebody go to all that trouble? Why would someone assume the identity of a man that multiple governments and any number of criminals would kill on sight?"

Hathaway shrugged. Then he asked Jake, "Computer matches and verification protocols aside, what's your gut telling you? Is that Ferrare?"

Jake took a deep breath. "It's not possible, and I don't know how it happened, but yeah. That's him."

"How sure are you?"

He looked Hathaway straight in the eye. "Dead sure."

Over the next week, Jake helped the H.O.T. Watch analysts subject the surveillance photos of Eduardo Ferrare to every verification test they could come up with. And the guy in the pictures passed every last one. With flying colors. The man in Gavarone *was* Eduardo Ferrare. How he'd survived the violent explosion that destroyed his house and charred his body to a crisp was a complete mystery. A phone call to his daughters verified that he wasn't a known twin—in fact, he had no living siblings to their knowledge. Both women also denied having heard from their father in the past five years. Given that he'd tried to kill them both and there was no love lost between parent and offspring, Jake was inclined to believe them.

Jake simply couldn't believe that Ferrare wasn't dead. Which meant this man had to be an exact double for the original. Or...the exact double had died in Joe Rodriguez's arms. Had they been outsmarted by the crime lord five years ago? If that was the case, what had the bastard been up to for all this time? Jake knew the man well enough to be certain it hadn't been anything good. Furthermore, if Ferrare was resurfacing now, it was for one reason and one reason only: some plan of the man's was about to come to fruition. The thought was chilling.

Jake had just finished working out and showering in the H.O.T. Watch facility's surprisingly well-equipped gym when his cell phone vibrated insistently. "Harrington here," he murmured.

"Jake. Brady. Can you come down to the conference room overlooking the Bat Cave?"

"On my way." He pocketed the phone and made his way down the stone tunnels left by the magma that had carved this place.

When he got to the conference room, all the senior management of the H.O.T. Watch was there. Brady Hathaway, his civilian counterpart, Jennifer Blackfoot, John Hollister, who commanded the Special Forces team attached to this unit, Carter Baigneaux, and a few other men he didn't recognize. They all had the hard, intelligent gazes of Special Forces operators, though.

He took the only free seat, halfway down the table. A closed brown folder—the kind mission assignments came in—lay on the table before him. But with his usual discipline, he didn't touch it. All in good time. But despite his exterior control, his gut twisted with anticipation. Was he finally going to get to finish the job his team had started over seven years ago?

Hathaway started without ceremony. "The Pentagon confirms our preliminary identification of Eduardo Ferrare."

Baigneaux sighed gustily in satisfaction at the far end of the table. Jake usually wasn't fond of demonstrative extroverts like

Carter, but it was hard not to like the guy and his infectious good humor. Of course, he was also damned proficient at what he did, and that went a long way toward making him okay in Jake's book.

"And we've had another development."

Jake looked up sharply. Hathaway's voice held just enough of an edge to send his adrenaline surging.

The Navy commander continued. "We've made another identification of a visitor to the Ferrare compound." He nodded to a computer tech and a photograph went up on the screen behind him. "This is General Fernando Alvarez. Number three guy in the Gavronese Army. In charge of drug interdictions and border patrol for the entire country. He was photographed entering the Ferrare compound at 2:45 a.m. nine days ago. He has not been seen since."

Not good. If the guy had tangled with Eduardo Ferrare, the good general was undoubtedly maggot fodder somewhere in the thick and plentiful jungles of Gavarone. They'd be lucky to find his skeleton someday to return to the widow.

Hathaway continued. "The powers that be feel that Alvarez's disappearance is grounds to take action. We've been authorized to send in a man to deal with the Ferrare problem directly. We were greenlighted to proceed with a covert insertion at 0230 hours Greenwich Mean Time tonight."

Jake glanced at his watch and made a quick time conversion. That was less than thirty minutes ago. And he was already getting a mission briefing? He had to give these H.O.T. Watch folks credit. They moved fast.

Opening his brown folder, Hathaway gestured for everyone else to do the same. Jake flipped his open. A photograph lay before him. It was an aerial view of the city block in St. George containing the compound in which Ferrare had been sighted. He'd already seen this picture and knew its general features.

"We are not tasked with finding Alvarez. Jennifer and I have succeeded in convincing our superiors that such a mission would be a waste of time and resources. We have, however, been ordered to put high-quality, close-range surveillance on Ferrare as soon as possible."

No surprise. A high-value target like Eduardo Ferrare, who had a history of orchestrating massive drug operations, would most definitely be the kind of man the United States wanted to keep tabs on. Particularly given his spectacular return from the dead.

"As far as we know, Ferrare has not been seen since the photographs of him were taken three weeks ago. However, we've had around-the-clock satellite surveillance on the place since, with only minor interruptions for cloud cover. We place the probability at well over ninety percent that he's still inside."

Jake knew all of this. The question was how was Hathaway planning to get eyes on the guy? Infiltrate the compound? A yardman or a cook, maybe? But knowing Ferrare, the guy would've handpicked even those people from only his most-trusted associates. The man had been nothing if not cautious before Charlie Squad supposedly killed him. Likely he'd be even more paranoid now.

It would have to be a standoff surveillance op, then. But the compound would be a pain to monitor. It was surrounded by a four-meter-tall stucco wall on all sides. Only one building nearby was high enough for anyone to see over, and that building was a stark, modern affair that wouldn't afford a spotter even the barest cover from its roof. Which left only...

"We have to put a man inside this apartment building," Hathaway said.

Jake nodded. Exactly. "Ferrare has undoubtedly identified that building as his only point of threat. I'd lay odds that everyone inside has been vetted out by his people. Thoroughly."

Jennifer Blackfoot smiled from her end of the table. The intelligence and violence in her gaze were impressive. The CIA operative was not a lady he'd want to tangle with in a dark alley. "Yes, but we've also done our homework. And we think we've found a crack in Ferrare's armor."

Jake's gut leaped with anticipation, but he replied blandly, "Do tell."

"This building is actually a condo complex. Each unit is privately owned, which means Ferrare doesn't have total control over who lives there. Turns out there's an American expatriate in the building on the fifth floor whose windows happen to face Ferrare's compound."

"Will he cooperate with us?" Jake asked.

"Not he. She. Shannon McMahon. Single. Schoolteacher. From a small Chicago suburb."

And she lived on her own in a city as violent as St. George? Gavarone had yet to stabilize after a bloody civil war a few years back. A civil war he and his teammates had had a front-row seat for, in fact. Jake asked, "What is she doing there? Teaching underprivileged kids or something?"

Jennifer shrugged. "We don't know. She has a surprisingly low electronic footprint. We're having to collect data on her the old-fashioned way…with human intelligence on the ground in St. George. It's going slow because we're having to tread lightly in that neighborhood. Based on what you've told us about Ferrare, Major Harrington, we're assuming Eduardo has plentiful spies and informants throughout the local area."

"Absolutely," Jake responded. "Have any of your people contacted her yet?"

"Not directly. Seems she's a bit of a recluse."

Carter commented wryly, "I would be, too, if I were an American woman living alone in that town."

Jake had to agree with the assessment. Hathaway was looking across the table at him, and he gazed back steadily, waiting.

"Any chance you're interested in taking point on this one, Jake? You know the target better than anyone else alive, except maybe his daughters."

He answered coldly, "I know him better than they do. And I'll recognize him at a distance far better than either of them would. I studied this guy until I knew him like my own mother." Although technically that was a lie. He had only the vaguest memory of her. His dad had taken him and left her when he was barely five years old and had raised him in the backwoods of Idaho. But the point was still valid.

"So. You want the job?"

He looked back at Hathaway levelly. "Ferrare's mine."

"I thought you might feel that way. Thing is, I need your head in the game on this one. No emotion. No vigilante justice. No payback for the crap he pulled on Charlie Squad way back when."

Jake cocked a single, sardonic eyebrow. "With all due respect, you're questioning *my* ability to be chilly?"

Chuckles sounded all around the table. Yeah. That was what he thought. He was the original man of ice, and they all knew it.

Hathaway shrugged, looking chagrined. "Sorry, buddy. I had to ask."

"Understood." Jake paused fractionally, then asked, "When do I leave?"

"Immediately."

"Oh. And one more question. What are my orders when I spot Ferrare?"

"Kill him."

Chapter 2

Shannon McMahon shoved a lock of her brunette hair out of her face to scowl at her white Persian cat luxuriating on the back of the sofa. "Stop shedding so much, Min. We've got hairballs on top of the hairballs around here. I swear, I'm going to give you away one of these days."

Mignette yawned, apparently bored with the whole subject. And then, to emphasize her dominion over the household, she commenced licking her back leg. And shedding more.

No matter how much she threatened, Shannon knew she wouldn't ever give the cat away, hair or no hair. She craved the companionship too much.

A quiet knock sounded at her front door and she jerked. *Deep breath. It's just someone at the door.* Probably Octavius, the very large, unabashedly gay Jamaican man who lived across the hall from her. She hadn't been in the market for a BFF when she moved here, but Octavius had appointed himself to the job of Best Friend Forever, and that was that.

"Coming!" Shannon called.

As always, she peered out the peephole before she opened the door. Whoa. Not Octavius. Alarm pounded through her veins, and suddenly she was huffing like a race horse. She peeked out again. Oh, God. This man looked mean. And scary. An impulse to hide nearly sent her bolting for her bedroom closet.

The man frowned and knocked again.

Go away, go away, go away. She held her breath for a solid minute, waiting for him to give up and leave. But he didn't. He stood there patiently, looking determined and stubborn. And scarier than ever.

Why wasn't he leaving? Then she remembered and winced. She'd called out that she was coming. Which pretty much ruled out pretending not to be home. She had to open the door.

Her hands started to shake. And then her knees joined in. She could do this. She checked the door chain to see that it was in place. And it was no flimsy apartment model. It was bolted into the wall frame and made with tempered steel links that could withstand three thousand pounds of pressure apiece.

She took a deep breath and turned the knob. She cracked the door open just far enough to peek out around the frame. "Can I help you?"

The man—Caucasian and wearing innocuous jeans, a polo shirt and a jacket—surprised her by answering in native English. "Miss McMahon? May I speak with you for a moment?"

"What do you want?" She made no move to open the door.

"Is there any chance we can speak inside?"

Her answer was quick and emphatic. "No."

He sighed. His voice lowered to a bare murmur. "I'm with

the United States government, ma'am. I need to speak to you in private."

Oh, God. It had happened. And this man had come to warn her.

"Please, Miss McMahon. This is official business. It's urgent."

No kidding. She muttered, "I need to see some identification."

"Of course." He reached with exaggerated slowness inside his leather jacket to a breast pocket and pulled out a wallet. He flipped it open and wedged out a green-and-white U.S. military ID card. He held it out for her inspection. Military? Not Justice Department?

She said, "Those are easy enough to fake. Have you got something better?"

One of his eyebrows cocked briefly, but he nodded and reached into his coat again. This time he brought out a brown, official U.S. passport. He held it open to his picture.

She stuck her hand through the narrow gap and snatched his passport out of his surprised grasp then stepped back from her door and examined the document. Jacob Harrington was the guy's name. He was thirty-four years old. His features were regular. Pleasant, even. In point of fact, he was a good-looking guy. It was just that his looks were so even, so homogenous, that it was easy to slide right over them and not even notice them. And for some reason, that creeped her out.

She registered more details. His hair was not quite buzzed and light brown. It accented the strong jaw and straight nose. Smooth, tanned skin stretched over cheekbones women would kill for. Yup, good-looking guy. On the other hand, his gray eyes looked up at her off the page in a way that didn't inspire trust. But then, she of all people knew that looks could be deceiving.

She stepped back to the crack in the door and was startled

to see him holding out several credit cards and a couple of photographs. A tattered library card topped the stack.

She glanced up, startled, and he smiled wryly at her. "Thought I'd save you the trouble of asking, ma'am."

Something about that smile galvanized her. It looked… rusty. Like he didn't use it much. Like it was an effort for him to produce it. She could relate to that. Time was, not so long ago, when she couldn't muster a smile, either.

He gave off an aura of being in control. Sure of himself. Ready and able to handle anything that came his way. It was oddly comforting. Like she didn't have to worry about anything when he was around. Either that, or he was going to squish her like a bug beneath his heel and there wasn't a darned thing she could do about it to save herself.

She frowned. She had to get over these sorts of thoughts. Not every man on the planet was a violent criminal, after all. Odds were this guy was perfectly decent and she was just being paranoid. As usual.

In sudden decision, she closed the door and reached for the chain. She could do this. She could let a man into her apartment without having a panic attack. She had a broom for a weapon, and she could always scream bloody murder. Octavius would be here in two shakes. And as long as that chain wasn't on her door, her linebacker-sized neighbor could burst in without any problem.

She swung the door open and took several steps back.

She watched warily as her guest stopped just inside the door and used his foot to push the door shut behind him. He put down two bulky, heavy-looking black duffel bags she hadn't seen before and raised his hands slowly away from his sides. "Ma'am, I'm not going to hurt you."

Famous last words… She checked herself. This guy hadn't done anything to threaten her. In fact, she was probably creeping him out. She sighed. "A woman can't be too careful, you know."

He nodded cautiously and said nothing.

"Would you like to sit down?" He wasn't that tall, maybe five foot ten or so, and lean. Still, the idea of him off his feet, not waiting threateningly to lunge at her, appealed to her.

He moved around the end of her couch and sat down on it, eyeing Mignette. "That's some big cat you've got there."

"Be careful of her. She hates strangers, and she's not declawed."

He reached out slowly and paused with his hand only perilous inches from Mignette's nose. A deep rumbling noise erupted, and Shannon watched in shock as her guest commenced stroking the purring feline. *Traitor!*

"Animals are usually comfortable with me," the man murmured. "What's his name?"

She sat down in the armchair by the window, well across the room from her guest. "*Her* name's Mignette. She's Persian. Some varieties can weigh up to twenty pounds."

He commented dryly, "I gather you don't have much of a mouse problem, then."

"She's been known to chase away large dogs, small ponies and the occasional deliveryman."

Harrington glanced up at her, startled. Belatedly, his mouth bent into one of those reluctant smiles of his.

"What brings you to St. George, Mr. Harrington?"

He did an odd thing. He went completely still. But it was more than that. It was like he sucked in the air and light around him until he almost wasn't in the room anymore.

"You do, ma'am. Or, rather, your apartment."

"My *apartment?*" Okay, that wasn't what she'd expected. She glanced around the colorful space with its terra-cotta floors and bright yellow walls. It was decidedly more cheerful and festively decorated than she felt at the moment. Some people would call her decorating choices overcompensation. Maybe they were right.

Her guest was speaking again in that end-of-the-world-serious voice of his. "I'm interested in your windows specifically. The view out of them."

"I beg your pardon?"

"Across the street. That large villa behind the wall. A man my employer is interested in may be staying there."

She frowned. "I don't pay any attention to the folks who come and go from that place. It gets a lot of visitors. I couldn't tell you who's there at the moment."

"I don't expect you to, ma'am. I'd like to have a look for myself."

"From my window?"

"Yes. If you don't mind."

It would bring him across the room. Closer to her. Her knuckles went white around the wood shaft. "Uhh, okay," she mumbled cautiously.

Thankfully, he moved slowly and headed for the far end of the big picture window. He plastered himself against the wall next to the glass, partially behind the bunched curtain. Slowly, he peered around the edge of the multicolored, striped fabric.

"What are you doing?" she asked curiously.

He answered without taking his eyes off the scene below. "I'm checking out the sight lines to the compound."

"What's a sight line?"

"Just like what it sounds like. It's an unobstructed view of a target or a target zone."

A *target?* That sounded dangerous! She half rose out of her chair in alarm. The movement caused his glance to snap over to her. She reeled at the cold calculation gleaming in his colorless gaze. Took a step backward. Stumbled on the edge of her area rug and took two more steps back from him. Must. Get. Away.

"Miss McMahon. I already told you. I'm not going to hurt you."

"Get out. Go. Now."

"Miss McMahon—"

"No! Leave! I'll scream. I'm warning you. I've had martial-arts training, and I'll defend myself. Violently."

His hands rose away from his sides again, palms up. He said slowly and clearly, "I swear. I will not harm you. You have my word of honor on it. "

"Words are cheap." No matter how fast she breathed, she couldn't quite catch her breath. Oh, Lord. She was panicking. No telling what she'd do if she lost control completely.

He sighed. "How about I go back to the couch and sit down again? Would that make you feel more comfortable?"

She nodded, too close to hyperventilating to speak.

He moved smoothly over to the sofa and sank down onto the cushions once more. She remained standing, hovering near her bedroom door. She could bolt for the bathroom. Get it locked before he could reach her. And then she could use the cell phone in her back pocket to call for help. A plan in place, she calmed slightly.

"Have you seen what you needed to see, Mr. Harrington? Can you go now?"

He sighed and pressed his lips tightly together. "Please call me Jake. Here's the thing, Miss McMahon. In order to answer your question, I'm going to have to reveal some sensitive information to you. It's highly classified, in fact. If you were to divulge any of this information to anyone, it could seriously impact the security of the United States. Hence, I have to ask you something first."

She stared. Was he for real? Classified information?

"Why did you leave the United States and come to a place like Gavarone?"

He met her gaze steadily, studying her intently. He looked serious. She replied reflectively, "I suppose it would seem a little strange for a single woman to come down here, wouldn't it? But that's the point."

"I beg your pardon?"

"I'm hiding. And who in their right mind would look for me here?"

"Are you in danger? Who's threatening you?"

If she wasn't mistaken, his voice had quickened with a hint of alarm. "Do you think I'd be living in St. George alone if I wasn't in danger?"

His mouth pursed faintly. You had to be watching this man carefully to catch the miniscule expressions and reactions that were all he displayed. His next question was entirely predictable, however.

"Who are you hiding from?"

"It's a long story, Mr.— Jake."

He lounged back and reached out one hand to pet Mignette. He looked prepared to settle in for as long as it took to hear the story. Not happening. It was a long, *private* story. She blurted, "I think you're the one who should be answering the questions here. Who are you looking for out my window?"

He leveled a long, measuring look at her. And then he surprised her by actually answering. "The man we're watching is a criminal. We thought he was dead, but we picked up satellite imagery that might be him. I've been assigned to confirm or dispel the rumor that he's still alive."

"Why look out my window at him? I thought satellites could read license plates from space."

"They can. But as good as cameras are, they still can't beat human eyes. I know this man very well. His mannerisms.

Gestures. The way he moves. A satellite camera can't capture that."

"And you know he's going to show himself in the next few minutes how?"

The faintest wrinkle of a frown flashed across his brow and disappeared. "I don't know that. My job is to get into place and wait for him to show himself."

She shot him a frown of her own. "And how long do you expect that to take?"

The shrug that lifted his shoulder was casual. "No idea."

"Give me an order of magnitude here. Are you talking a few hours or all day?"

Amusement flickered in his gaze. "If we're lucky."

"And if we're not?"

"Several days. Weeks. No way to tell."

Her jaw dropped. "You want to stand in my living room and look out my window for weeks?"

"If that's what it takes."

Only the flat calm with which he said that kept her from laughing aloud. "You've got to be kidding!" she burst out.

"No, I'm not."

"No. No way. No man's moving into my apartment with me. And certainly not a man like you—" She broke off abruptly.

When she didn't continue, he visibly sighed. "What's wrong with me?"

"You're strong. And fit. And…" The word that came to mind was threatening. "And I don't know you," she finished lamely.

"I won't bother you. Not much, at any rate. I'll park in the corner and stay out of your way as best I can."

And she was supposed to just ignore a full-grown man in her place? Not happening. She shook her head in the negative.

"Ma'am, this is a matter of national security. I'll give you the phone number and e-mail of my headquarters. Or call the American Embassy downtown. You can verify my identity with them."

She shook her head again.

"Miss McMahon. I'm the only person who knows this guy well enough to make the identification. I *have* to do this. My only other option is to go up on the roof of your building and try to hide from this criminal and his men. And your roof is as flat as a pancake. They'll spot me in a day or two and pick me off with a sniper of their own. My mission will fail, not to mention I'll die, if you don't let me do this surveillance from in here."

He sounded more concerned about the mission than his death. And something moved deep inside her in recognition. She remembered all too well the days when she'd wanted nothing more than to die but hadn't had the courage to end it all. In retrospect, she was glad she hadn't killed herself. But at the time…she'd been certain there was no way out of the abyss. Was this man lost in his own black void, his own private hell of the human soul? Intuitive certainty filled her that it was so.

An urge to reach out to him, to show him the way back, startled her.

"Tell you what," she said in sudden decision. "You can use my apartment for as long as it takes to spot your guy. I'll go bunk in with a friend until you're done."

Jake shook his head decisively. "Won't work. My target will have spies on every floor of this place watching the comings and goings of everybody. You need to go on living your regularly scheduled life out of your own apartment, or it'll tip off his men that something's up."

"Then how did you get to my door with those big bags and nobody noticing you?"

He frowned. "I came up the service elevator from the back entrance and spent under a minute outside your door. It's a calculated risk, but odds are no one saw me. And you can always tell anyone who asks that you had some work done on your place. If, however, I were to make a habit of moving around your building for days or weeks, I would surely be spotted and reported."

"So you also want me to act as your cover?"

"I *need* you to act as my cover, ma'am."

"You seriously think you can waltz into my life, announce that you're moving into my apartment, and oh, by the way, I have to risk my life to help you?"

He met her gaze head-on. "I'm sorry. But that's pretty much the way it is."

"You're out of your mind."

"I wish I were."

For a moment, just a moment, she was tempted by his proposition. When she wasn't busy being terrified of him, he was actually sort of gorgeous. And she had to give him credit. So far he'd been polite, respectful and had done nothing threatening. But she knew all too well how that could change on a dime. She just couldn't do it. The idea of going to sleep with a strange man in her house... Oh, no. No, no.

She opened her mouth to turn him down, but he cut her off. "What are you so afraid of? What do you think I'm going to do to you?"

Afraid? Her? The accusation stung all the more because it was true. Dammit, she'd succumbed to the fear again. She tried and tried, but she couldn't quite conquer the beast.

She replied more tartly than she otherwise might have. "For all I know, you've got a gun in the bag, and you're planning to worm your way into my home, wait till I'm asleep and attack me."

"Ahh." He gave her a considering look. "Well, if that's what you're worried about, let's get that out of the way now."

He came at her so fast she barely had time to throw up her hands before he was on her. The panic exploded then, in a blinding white flash inside her skull. She froze for just an instant...and then she went berserk.

She threw kicks and elbows and scratches every which way. All the careful self-defense moves she'd been taught went right out the window, and she fought like a wild thing.

Not that it did a bit of good. He actually laughed at her. Then he slipped away from her—she didn't have any idea how—and had the gall to lecture her!

"You civilians. You don't understand what it means to fight to the death. You're not willing to take the collateral damage—the pain—to win. That's why people like me always defeat people like you."

Stung, she redoubled her efforts, but to no avail. He merely lunged forward smoothly and wrapped his arms around her, tightening them like bands of steel, trapping her arms between them. Her palms shoved against a chest wrapped in slabs of hard, heretofore unnoticed, muscle. He leaned forward, arching her backward, throwing her off balance until she was actually forced to cling to him. His shoulder muscles were no less powerful than the rest of him.

In her mind, another set of strong muscles loomed over her in another darkened room. Bigger and meatier, but just as effective. She was helpless again, tied to her bed, at the mercy of a monster who laughed to see her pain. Mad. Sadistic. With black, inhuman eyes.

Icy silver eyes, as light as the others had been dark, captured her unfocused gaze, forcing her back to this moment. This attack. Where she expected to see pleasure and rage in that gaze, there was only cold calm. Maybe even a hint of sadness. And that was what pulled her back from the brink of hysteria now. The monster in her nightmares had neither compassion nor control. But this man did.

Nonetheless, she was still under attack, and she'd be damned if any man pushed her around again. Ever. She renewed her struggles, determined to free herself. To hurt this guy before he could hurt her. To go down fighting this time.

Inexorably his grasp tightened even more, crushing her struggles into ineffective squirms, and then into little more than labored breaths. This must be what a rabbit felt like in the coils of a python. Spots danced in front of her eyes, and she began to feel light-headed. She was going to be seriously pissed if she fainted and he ended up doing whatever he wanted to her.

But before she could actually pass out, he lifted her with depressing ease and dropped her facedown on the couch. His arms loosened, and she fought back immediately. But he tightened his grip again, this time using his body weight also to crush her deep into the cushions.

"You're making it damned hard not to hurt you," he growled.

Huh?

"Are you done freaking out?" He ground out the words in her ear.

She tried to throw him off her, to no avail.

He sprawled on top of her and used his strength and weight to contain her until she finally subsided. She wasn't surrendering for a second. But for now, she would bide her time and wait for her opening to strike back. To win her freedom and her life. Oh, yes. She knew how to play this game. Time to play possum.

He spoke calmly. "There. Now that we've established that I can do that, I'm going to let you go. And now you won't have to get all worked up imagining it happening and letting your fears get the best of you. I give you my word I won't ever do that again."

Before she could hardly make sense of all that, he did the damnedest thing. *He let her go.* He pushed up and away from her with a quick bunching of muscles. His heat and weight and hands were gone. She was free.

She rolled off the couch and to her feet in a feral crouch with her hands clawed in front of her, ready to attack again.

She stopped. And stared. He was just straightening up over one of his bags. And in his right hand was a gun.

Sick defeat washed over her. *Game over.* She froze in indecision. Jump at him and force him to shoot her now, or hang on to hope for a little while longer and try to escape or draw attention and bring help?

While she debated it, he strode forward. And stopped an arm's length away from her.

He growled, "I can't believe I'm doing this. But it looks like this is the only way I'm going to make this mission happen. Here. Take it."

She frowned up at him then looked down at his hand. He was holding the gun out to her, butt first.

Chapter 3

Jake waited patiently for her to take the weapon. She looked up at him with huge, frightened eyes, so blue they almost hurt to look at and fringed by the blackest, longest lashes he'd ever seen. She reminded him of a wild creature too wounded to run from a predator and reduced to begging in silent futility for its life. What had made her this afraid? Or who? For surely only a human had the cruelty to terrify another living creature this badly.

Just as surely, it had to have been a man. Disgust for whoever had done this to her surged through him. Sometimes it was an embarrassment to be a member of the male half of the human race.

Her gaze darted back down to the pistol. Eventually, she reached out and took the weapon, but hesitantly enough that it was clear she was neither familiar with nor a fan of firearms. Which did nothing to inspire confidence in him. Weapons in the hands of an amateur, particularly a terrified female he'd just attacked, were a recipe for disaster.

But what other choice did he have? She was so busy fantasizing the worst, she could hardly see straight. It had been a gamble to give her exactly what she feared. The next few seconds would tell the tale of whether or not forcing her to face her fear would pay off.

It was what he'd have done if she were a soldier freaking out over some imagined terror. No telling if it would work on a civilian or whether the shock of it would be too much for her. Thing was, he had no idea what else to do. He didn't know the first thing about girly-girl females like this one.

She gazed down at the pistol and back up at him. "Who *are* you?" she whispered.

"I told you. I'm a U.S. military officer, and I need to use your apartment to do surveillance on a criminal who may be holed up across the street. And unfortunately, I need your help to pull it off. This will never work until you get over being scared of me."

"And you think *attacking* me will inspire confidence in me?" she burst out.

"Have you got any better ideas? Would you actually believe me if I gazed deep into your eyes and declared sincerely how honorable a soul I am and how much I respect women?"

Her snort said it all. *As I'd thought.*

She backed up until her calves banged into her original chair—a bright red thing that swallowed her and left her looking pale and small. He had a hard time believing this place was actually decorated to reflect her taste. She seemed more the white lace and pastels type. Her ruffled skirt and lace-collared blouse were more in keeping with his first impression of her.

She sat down heavily, the gun cradled in her lap. She seemed less skittish when he wasn't on his feet so he sat back down on the couch. Maybe she didn't like people looming over her. He wasn't that tall, a shade under six feet, but she was a tiny little thing. She was all but overpowered by her glossy black hair, brilliant blue eyes, and fair skin. Black Irish if he had to guess. As pretty a lass as he'd ever laid eyes on, too. And as scared as he'd ever seen a person.

Fear had vibrated through every part of her, like blood flowing through her veins, as he'd lain on top of her. It had been a struggle not to loosen his grip and gather her close to him in comfort, soothing away her terror. He hadn't been that close to a woman in…hell, he couldn't remember the last time.

The need that had exploded through him then still pounded through his veins now. It wasn't about sex—well, at least mostly, it wasn't. It was more fundamental than that. It was about simple human contact. He craved skin on skin. Shared body heat. The feel of another pulse against his. A reminder that he was *alive*.

But that was not for him. He killed people. He didn't snuggle with them.

Still, an urge to go to her, to kneel before her and coax her into his arms, nearly overcame him. He could close his eyes and imagine the feel of her. He could already smell the innocence on her skin and sunshine in her hair….

He jerked his attention back to the present. He suspected the slightest display of interest in her on his part would earn her everlasting hatred—and blow this mission straight to hell. And he would deserve her hatred. He might be a killer, but he wasn't the kind of bastard who took advantage of a terrified woman.

This woman's paranoia was off the charts. Which made it all the more inexplicable that she was living in St. George, with its long-standing reputation as one of the most violent cities in the western hemisphere. The unrest seething in the streets earlier today was nearly as bad as the first time he'd ever come to Gavarone, five years ago, when a civil war had broken out.

Who could have scared this woman so bad that she'd hide in a place hovering on the brink of civil war rather than risk being found?

He checked the thought. It wasn't his problem. He was here to do a job and get out of Dodge. Nothing more. He was not in the business of doing gratuitous psychotherapy on single, civilian women who happened to be acting as his convenient cover.

She announced, "I'm calling my neighbor. I want him to check you out."

Alarm coursed through him. "No!" That was the *last* thing he needed. As it was, a heavy sense of claustrophobia hung over him. Death and mission failure would follow shortly if he was spotted by anyone while this close to Ferrare. All it would take was for one of Ferrare's spies in this building to grow the slightest bit suspicious.

If he or Shannon took the slightest misstep, they were both dead. Not a reassuring thought, given this woman's fragile and volatile frame of mind. Although frankly, he'd be hard-pressed to trust even a hard-headed and entirely sane woman right about now. He definitely didn't need to add any of her neighbors to the mix.

Her eyes narrowed immediately in suspicion.

He explained hastily. "This is the only structure with a sight line over that wall and into the compound across the street. Eduardo Ferrare—he's the guy I'm hoping to see—has no doubt got spies and informants in this building. And there's no way to tell who they are. *Nobody* can know I'm here."

"But Octavius is okay—"

"Did you grow up with him? Is he too wealthy to bribe?

Does he have no family that could be used against him? Does he have a high-level American security clearance?"

"Well, no, but—" she stuttered.

"Then you can't be sure he's not on Ferrare's payroll. It's not that he's working directly for the guy, mind you. Somebody could just slip him an envelope of cash now and then, and in return, he keeps an eye on his neighbors. Any chance this Octavius of yours is the chatty type? Nosy? Knows everyone in the building and makes it his business to know everything about everyone?"

The appalled look on her expressive face was answer enough.

"Will you allow me to stay here and do my surveillance?"

No surprise, she didn't answer right away. They sat in silence for several minutes and he left her to her thoughts. She was prettier than the surveillance photos of her he'd been shown. But then, in the pictures she'd been hunched down into her clothes and slinking along shop fronts like a mouse afraid to be seen. She wasn't the kind of woman who turned heads the moment she walked into a room. She was more the kind whose beauty grew on you the longer you looked at her. It was subtle. In the lines of her cheek and jaw. The tilt of her head on her graceful neck. The innocent sweetness in her gaze when she wasn't frozen in terror.

And her eyes…so transparent. So readable. Her heart and everything in it was right there for a man to see. Whereas he'd made a lifetime study of concealing everything about himself and his thoughts from others, she was the polar opposite. If he was a brick wall, she was an open window.

Finally, she sighed. A flicker of triumph coursed through him at the sound of capitulation.

"It is for my country," she said reluctantly. "And it's not

like you can do anything to me that I haven't already been through."

Were it not for his years of intense self-discipline, his jaw would have dropped open. *What in the hell had happened to this woman?* At his first opportunity, he was going to insist that H.O.T. Watch do a full background check on her and find out exactly what had made her so fearful of men and so resigned to violence.

In the meantime, he was flying blind here. All he knew was that he was trapped in a tiny apartment with a woman who was far from stable. Oh, and his life depended entirely on her cooperation. Great. Just great.

How he was going to keep her from doing something stupid before he could get out of here was anyone's guess. He swore under his breath. This was why civilians were such a damned nightmare to work with. The op was already going down the tubes, and he hadn't even been here ten minutes.

It was clear from both expression and body language that Shannon couldn't believe she'd just agreed to take him in. Frankly, after seeing the degree of her fear, he couldn't believe she'd agreed to it, either. He hated having to bully her into it. But he had no choice. There was no other way to get the job done. The rainy season was fast approaching, and satellite surveillance had its limitations, cloud cover being one of them.

"Did you have to jump me like that?" she demanded without warning, disrupting his train of thought.

He winced mentally. "It seemed necessary."

"You scared me to death!"

A pang of genuine regret stabbed him. "I'm sorry about that. I wouldn't have done it if I knew of any other way."

He braced himself for her to ream him out, but she only sighed. "My therapist had to shock me out of panic attacks a few times. I just wasn't expecting it from you."

Therapist? Wasn't that spiffy? She was crazy, too. But then protectiveness surged in his gut. His old man had been as crazy as a loon, and as a kid he'd managed well enough living with the bastard. Until his father finally killed himself in a drunken depression. So. Whatever had made Shannon fearful had been bad enough to drive her into counseling, huh? A need to find out who'd hurt her and make that person pay for it rolled through Jake.

Whoa. Easy, Tarzan. This particular Jane didn't need a macho he-man charging to her rescue. In fact, macho he-men seemed to scare the living hell out of her. Problem was, he was a soldier honed to a killing edge, and nothing was going to change that.

He had to actively fight temptation to take the opening she'd given him and ask who or what had made her so afraid. But caution won out. He had no doubt she'd panic and bolt if he pushed her the slightest bit.

Silence fell between them again.

Absently, he stroked the cat. Loud purring filled the silence and clouds of white hair floated up around the beast. *Patience, old man.* Thankfully, that was something he was very good at. He settled in to wait for as long as it took Shannon to work through the demons dancing in her troubled gaze.

Eventually, she stirred in her chair. In a small voice, she said, "Now what?"

"Now I set up my surveillance equipment and get to work, while you get on with your usual life."

She sighed. "I was sweeping up Mignette's hair when you knocked. That cat sheds like no creature I've ever seen before."

He'd noticed. It was hard not to. He said gently, "I'm going to go over to my bags and pull out some electronic equipment. Is that okay?"

She looked surprised that he asked. Only belatedly did she

nod. He eased to his feet, vividly aware of the 9 mm Beretta in her lap. His shoulder blades itched as he turned his back on the weapon. As he started rummaging through his gear and setting the first pieces he'd need on the floor, he spied something and pulled it out gratefully.

He rose and turned around in one smooth movement. She was still sitting in her chair, staring down at the gun in her lap. He asked quietly, "Would you like a holster to put that in?"

"Uhh, I guess so."

He walked across the living room and held the leather harness out. "You put your arms through these two loops and adjust this buckle across your back. Then the pistol slips into the holster under your left arm. You're right-handed, aren't you?"

"How did you know?"

"When I pushed you down to the couch, you used your right hand to catch yourself. Plus, you slugged me harder with that hand."

She scowled.

To distract her from getting worked up again over his attack, he said, "See that lever on the side of the weapon by your index finger? That's the safety. If you swing it up, perpendicular to the gun's barrel, the weapon can't fire. Parallel to the barrel, and it's ready to go. Just aim and pull the trigger. It'll automatically chamber another round after you fire. And if you do shoot, hang on tight. It'll buck hard in your hand."

Her blue eyes went black as her pupils dilated.

He sighed. "There's no need to fear a gun. Respect it, yes. But it's only a tool. The human on the business end of any weapon is the one you need to worry about."

She nodded, hard knowledge of that truth written in her gaze, and his knuckles itched to pummel somebody on her behalf. He cleared his throat. "Want me to help you put the holster on?"

She started to nod, started to stand. Then stopped herself. "Why are you being nice to me? What do you want from me?"

Ahh. The lady equated nice to manipulation. He answered gruffly, "I'm not being nice. I'll feel a lot safer if that thing's stowed where you can't drop it and hurt either one of us."

She jolted. "Could it go off if I drop it?"

"Nah. But let's not take any chances, eh?"

She actually turned around and presented her back to him so he could slip the holster straps up her arms. The fledgling trust it demonstrated inexplicably warmed his gut. Or maybe she was just too naive to realize the vulnerable position she'd put herself into. He was careful not to touch her skin as he ran the straps up her slender arms but not for want of an errant desire to do so.

Her hair smelled good. He leaned closer to catch the clean scent. Something lightly citrus with a tang of…ginger. *Holster, dammit.* He reached for the buckle and fumbled at the leather. Fumbled? Him? The virtuoso sniper whose eye-hand coordination confounded most mortals' imaginations? His knuckles bumped into her back. Through the thin cotton knit of her shirt, her body was warm. He felt the shiver between her shoulder blades at his touch. Aww, jeez. She was as responsive as she looked.

He stepped back, feeling big and awkward all of a sudden. An odd sensation for him. "Uhh, lemme get back to my gear. You just…do whatever you'd usually do."

"Somehow, I don't see myself crawling around on my hands and knees sweeping under the sofa for hairballs with this thing on." She gestured at the gun now nestling under her left armpit, snuggled up against the curve of her breast.

The gun looked big and ugly, massively out of place on

her petite frame. At a loss for anything to say, he returned to his gear bag. Carefully, he lifted out a bulky, bubble-wrapped bundle and set it on the floor.

"What's that?"

He glanced up at her. "Flowerpots. You're going to need to buy some plants the next time you go out."

"Whatever for?"

"To disguise my surveillance gear." He reached for his ankle sheath and pulled out his switchblade. When he pushed the release button, six inches of wicked steel flipped up. He started to cut the wrapping away, but then he noticed a pair of blue eyes blazing in fury across the room like twin blowtorches. And they were glaring at him down the barrel of his gun.

He froze as death's cold fingers crept up his neck. "What the—" He looked down at the blade in his hand. "Oh. It's just my utility knife."

She looked furious. "It's a weapon. I want you to get rid of every weapon you've got."

He frowned. "That's going to be a problem, ma'am. Almost everything in your apartment is a weapon to me."

"Huh?" She looked around, confused.

"I can use the sofa to suffocate someone. The wall to smash someone's head. I know exactly where and how hard to stab that ballpoint pen on your kitchen counter into the base of someone's skull to kill them. That book on the coffee table can crush a larynx. Hell, the magazine beneath it can be rolled up and put out someone's eye. And then there are my hands and feet. They're technically lethal weapons, too."

She was shaking her head, and that haunted look was back in her eyes. "This isn't going to work."

He sighed. "Yes. It will. We'll find a way. Hang in there with me, Miss McMahon. I just need a little time to prove to you that you can trust me."

She snapped, "You might as well call me Shannon if we're going to be living together."

If only. She was the kind of woman a man could get used to playing house with real easily. Meanwhile, time was a wasting, and there were still no eyes on the compound across the street.

"Is there somewhere you can lock yourself in while I get all this gear set up? I'm going to be using my knife and running wires, and messing with big, scary tripods for about an hour."

"I'm not scared of tripods."

"You should be. I could knock someone's head off with one if I had to."

She shuddered. And beat a tactical retreat into her bedroom. He didn't hear a lock immediately. Must've gone to her bathroom to lock herself in.

With her and her fragile emotional state finally out of the way, he made short work of setting up his equipment. He set up six cameras and trained one on each window and door of the main house across the street. He pointed two more cameras at the front and side gates through the outer wall. Each of his lenses was cleverly hidden in the black-and-white pattern painted on the flowerpots. Each one was also equipped with motion detectors that would automatically start sending wireless video images to his laptop computer any time they detected movement of any kind.

He aligned the pots in a row on her windowsill, ran the wires behind the curtains, down the wall and into the big armoire in the corner, which he appropriated for his recording equipment. He bored a small hole in the back of the armoire with his knife and ran the various wires through it. Hopefully, Shannon wouldn't have a cow if she discovered his vandalism.

In a few minutes, the cameras were up and running. Now, any time the sensors recorded movement, he'd hear a warning beep in the wireless earpiece he'd inserted in his left ear, and a video feed would be sent to his computer and to the writeable DVD system inside the armoire.

He set up his laptop on the rustic dining table at the end of the living room near the kitchen, established a wireless connection with the cameras and opened windows on his screen, one for each video feed. The white stucco of the compound across the street leapt onto his screen from a bunch of different angles.

The reality of sitting nearly on top of one of the most dangerous men on the planet slammed into him. And an innocent woman was in the next room, her life as much at risk now as his was.

Come to papa, you bastard. Eduardo had slipped through the net for the last time.

Jake called out, "I'm done, Shannon. My weapons of mass destruction are stowed, if you want to come out."

She didn't respond immediately, and he didn't push the matter. He spent a few minutes familiarizing himself with the angles of each view and orienting himself with which camera was looking at what.

A sharp vibration in his pocket sent him fishing for his cell phone. He looked at the number on the display. H.O.T. Watch Ops. "Go ahead," he muttered.

"It's Jennifer. How's it going?"

"I'm in. Got the cameras up and running about two minutes ago. I'll be ready to test the satellite feed to you guys momentarily."

"How's Miss McMahon?"

"Funny you should ask," he said in a low voice. "Let's just say the lady's not the slightest bit pleased with the arrangement."

"Yeah, well, I may be able to shed a little light on why that's so."

"Do tell."

"Our research team's been digging on her. Turns out she's got a Justice Department file."

"What for?" he blurted, startled.

"We don't know. It's sealed. We're gonna have to go through the U.S. Attorney General's office to get permission to unseal the thing. We only know it was a criminal case about seven years ago. "

"Was she the victim?"

"No idea."

"How long till you know more?"

"Dunno. We're working on the paperwork as fast as we can. Maybe we can get someone to review the request late tonight. Most likely it'll be tomorrow."

"Hurry, will ya?"

"What's the rush?"

He heard the bedroom door knob turn. "Just do it. Gotta go." He disconnected the call.

"Who were you talking to?" Shannon asked, her face the picture of wide-eyed innocence.

Damn, she looked as pure as a newborn lamb. So unlike him in every way. He'd long ago lost his last vestiges of anything vaguely resembling innocence. He'd seen—hell, he'd done—the very worst human beings were capable of. He'd taken the lives of others. Eighty-four of them, to be precise. Enough to fill two buses.

He knew not only their names but their faces. Friends. Hobbies. Eating habits. The last thing they'd been doing before they died. Hell, their last facial expression. And he also recalled the red mist that had been left behind as he blew the heads off of every last one of them.

No matter what sins lurked in the past of Shannon McMahon in that sealed Justice Department file, he'd unquestionably done worse. Still, if he was going to complete the mission, he needed to know the details. Surely she wasn't a perpetrator, but rather a victim. Everything about her shouted frightened woman who'd been terrorized by some sick monster. Still, he could be wrong.

His gut twisted. He wanted to believe the best of her. His instincts yelled at him to do so. But he dared not. After all, he'd handed her his gun.

Chapter 4

Shannon puttered around the kitchen making a complete hash of cooking lunch. Her hands kept shaking, and her attention kept straying to the man seated statuelike at her dining-room table staring intently at his laptop computer. She narrowly missed dumping an entire bottle of orange juice on the floor and charred the first grilled-cheese sandwich to a blackened crisp. Meanwhile, Jake didn't move a muscle. It was eerie bordering on creepy how still he was.

"You want something to eat?" she eventually called out.

He looked up, startled, like he'd been in some kind of trance. "Uhh, sure."

"Don't you want to know what I made?"

He shrugged.

She succumbed to an impulse to get a rise out of him. "The big local delicacy is jellied squid with chili-lime sauce."

"Yeah. I know."

Dang. The guy said that as dry and deadpan as the desert. "Want some?"

"Got some?" he retorted.

She poked her head out of the kitchen. She'd like to scowl at him for calling her bluff but ended up laughing instead. "No. But I can buy some the next time I go to the grocery store."

His mouth twitched briefly, which was, as far as she could tell, his version of a smile. Maybe someday she'd get lucky and hear the guy actually laugh. She carried in a plate of grilled-cheese sandwiches, a bowl of sliced melon, and made a return trip to the kitchen for iced tea.

"Expecting someone else for lunch?" he asked.

She glanced at the heaping platter of sandwiches then ventured to look back up at him. That might just be a spark of humor behind that unfathomable silver gaze. "I didn't know how much you'd eat," she confessed.

He shrugged. "Depends."

"On what?" She sat down across from him and helped herself to a sandwich.

"On what I'm doing. If I'm lying in a hide, I might not eat for a couple of days. If I'm prepping to do a long run for physical training, I'll load up to ten thousand calories of carbs over the course of a day."

Ten thousand—holy smokes. "What's a hide?"

He replied blandly, "Sometimes I'm sent out to watch people and there's not a pleasant apartment across the street with a cooperative American citizen in it. A hide is just that. I find a place where I won't be spotted and hide so I can watch whoever I'm supposed to."

Her teacher radar for a lie fired and told her he was tap-dancing around something. She probed cautiously. "You watch people for a living?"

"Something like that."

Right. And she was born yesterday. He did sneaky stuff. Spy stuff.

He picked up a sandwich, and she was startled to notice how small it looked in his hands as he took a bite. His fingers moved gracefully, but the power in them—in all of him, for that matter—was unmistakable. She didn't know whether to be appalled or thrilled; but either way, she couldn't tear her fascinated gaze away from the mesmerizing dance of his nimble fingers as he ate the meal.

She noticed other details about him as she watched. His teeth were white and strong. His jaw muscles rippled faintly when he chewed. And when he swallowed, watching the muscles in his throat work did the darnedest things to her stomach. He ate as quietly and efficiently as he did everything else: unhurried, but with purpose. Did he make love that way—whoa. Cancel that thought.

He was a scary, strange man who'd barged into her apartment without warning to spy on some guy out her window and likely do violence against him. That was not the equation for attractive males in her world. Exactly the opposite, in fact. An image of a massive black shape landing on top of her in her bed, waking her from a dead sleep to a nightmare beyond her worst imagining, flashed into her head. The familiar iron band of terror tightened around her chest until she thought she'd pass out. *Breathe. In. Count to three. Out...*

"You okay?" he asked.

Darn him. Too observant for his own good.

"Yeah," she managed to get out past the panic tightening her throat. She had to distract herself. Think about something else before she completely lost it. She cast her mind about frantically for a new topic. She blurted, "What constitutes a long training run in your world?"

"Seventy or eighty miles."

Her jaw sagged. "You can run that far all at once?"

"We don't do it often, and it's not like we're sprinting. But it's good to know you can go that far if you have to."

Who in the heck was this guy?

They finished their lunch in silence. He seemed perfectly at ease with that, but it felt weird to her to eat an entire meal with another person and say absolutely nothing. She would definitely classify the silence as awkward.

But then he broke it abruptly. "I need to use the restroom, and I gather there's only one in this condo. Is this going to be a problem for you?"

She blinked up at him in surprise. "What are you going to do if I say it is? It's not like you can run across the hall and use the neighbor's, right?"

He sighed. "I don't know what I'd do. I'd figure something out. Wear diapers, maybe. I'm trying not to freak you out here."

Him? In diapers? She fought to contain a laugh. "You may use the bathroom. As long as I'm not in it, feel free."

He got up from the table, an exercise in silent, lethal grace, and headed for her bedroom. "Lock the door when you use it, okay?"

She stared at his retreating back askance at that advice, but heard nothing other than a desire not to walk in on her by accident. This guy was trying awfully hard to put her at ease. Were it not for the fact that he'd already had her pinned beneath him on the couch and could've done whatever he wanted to her then, she'd be convinced he was just trying to get her to let her guard down so he could move in for the kill.

She leaned over to pick up his plate, and the pistol poked her underarm uncomfortably. How did all those federal agents who'd worn these things around her do it? Her thoughts hitched. *Of course.* Why hadn't she thought of that earlier?

With a furtive glance toward her bedroom door, she raced into the kitchen and picked up her cell phone. She scrolled through her address book until she found the name she was looking for and dialed it quickly. The phone at the other end rang. She glanced over her shoulder fearfully, checking to make sure Jake was still in the bathroom. *C'mon, c'mon. Pick up already.*

"Agent Watson."

Shannon talked fast. "Hey, Crystal, it's Shannon McMahon. I need a favor. Could you find out about a guy named Jacob Harrington for me? He's supposedly in the military. An army major, I think. Is he for real?"

"What am I? Your dating referral service?" the federal marshal groused, laughing. "Hi, Shannon. How are you?"

"A little weird at the moment, actually."

"What's up?"

"Can't say right now."

The woman at the other end of the line waxed tense and businesslike. "Are you in danger? Do I need to send in help?"

"No to both, I think."

"Can you speak freely?"

Shannon sighed. She hadn't intended to set off DEFCON 1 with her request. "Really, Crystal. I'm fine. I just…met a guy…and I want to know…"

"If he's feeding you a line or if he's who he says he is?" Crystal finished for her.

"Well, yeah."

"A man? You? Will wonders never cease? It's about time, kiddo. Seven years is too long to pull yourself out of the dating scene. Get back on the horse, I say."

"The horse didn't torture and assault you and nearly kill you."

The agent's voice dropped to a sympathetic timbre. "You're

right. Ignore me and my big mouth, hon. I fully understand your impulse to check this guy out. I've got a meeting to go to, but I'll run a quick background check on him as soon as I get back to my desk. I'll call you in an hour. I promise."

"You're a peach, Crystal," Shannon replied in relief. She ended the call and stuffed the phone back in her pocket. Hastily, she started doing the dishes.

"Can I help with those?" The male voice came from directly behind her, and Shannon about jumped out of her skin. She whirled around, and Jake was already stepping back rapidly, his hands held wide, away from his sides.

"I'm sorry," he murmured. "I didn't mean to startle you. I'll try to make more noise the next time I approach."

Her heart slammed against her ribs at double speed until the deep, calming breaths she'd been taught for managing panic attacks started to kick in. The way he moved triggered her internal alarm system. He was too darned predatory for her peace of mind. She was starting to feel like a lamb locked in a closet with a wolf. And come to think of it, he did sort of look like a wolf with those silver eyes and the watchful, hungry look in them.

Belatedly, she muttered, "I'll do the dishes."

He moved across the living room and parked himself behind her curtains like he had earlier. He did the statue thing again and all but faded into her wall. She left him to his Zen state and went back into the kitchen to finish cleaning up. He was still standing in exactly the same position she'd left him when she emerged fifteen minutes later. The guy was definitely too intense for her.

She retreated to her bedroom with a book and locked the door behind her. She curled up on the bed and tried to read, but it was futile. When she was nervous, she needed to be in motion. She straightened and dusted her bedroom from top to bottom and scrubbed her bathroom until it sparkled, which managed to pass the next hour. Crystal still hadn't called, though, so she started on her closet, reorganizing her clothes until they were so neat they'd pass a military inspection.

Another half hour passed, and still Crystal hadn't called. The panic started to creep up on her again. What had the agent found out about her mystery guest that was delaying her like this? Oh, heck. Crystal's meeting had probably just run long. She was making a mountain out of a molehill. But after another half hour passed, Shannon's gut seriously started to gnaw at her.

She'd gone back to her book and forced her gaze to travel across a few more pages as the clock ticked away and her phone remained frustratingly silent. What was going on? Why hadn't Crystal called back by now? She'd never known the agent to break a promise. *Oh, God. What was wrong with Jake Harrington?*

Boredom wasn't a state Jake registered anymore on a job. He'd spent so many years doing absolutely nothing, staring at absolutely nothing, that it was his usual state of working existence. With one part of his mind he observed his target, but with another part of it he thought about all sorts of things, from books he'd read to current political events to reviewing training procedures. He actually found long surveillance missions like this relaxing.

Maybe he was a little too relaxed after that tasty lunch and pleasant company, though, because when his laptop beeped a warning in his ear, it caught him by surprise. He almost always spotted threats before the electronic sensors he used to supplement his hides, but today he was caught completely flat-footed. He scanned the compound below frantically. There. A tiny black tube protruding from the far corner of the main house.

Damn! Infrared scanner. And it was pointed at this building, quartering it methodically.

Jake took off running, tearing across the living room and blasting through Shannon's bedroom door. In the second it took him to race a few frantic strides to her bed, she barely had time to lurch upright, for her book to fall out of her hands. But it was long enough for complete and utter horror to break across her face.

He leaped.

Her mouth opened as she drew breath to scream.

He slammed into her, landing on top of her and slapping a heavy hand across her mouth all in one movement. And he might as well have been wrestling a hellcat.

"Shannon," he grunted as she thrashed hysterically beneath him, "I'm not going to hurt you."

Her fist slammed into the side of his head, and he saw stars.

"Infrared sensors!" he explained urgently. She heaved, trying to toss him off, and he splayed his legs wide in a wrestling stance to hold her pinned beneath him. She turned her head violently side to side, trying to throw off his hand. He dared not let her scream, though. The neighbors would hear and call the police.

"Calm, down, Shannon! Oww! I swear, I'm not going to hurt you!" But it was a damn good bet someone had hurt her before, given the way she was freaking out. Her knee yanked up and he took a crotch shot that had him gasping as badly as she was.

Teeth gritted against pain that would've brought him to his knees had he been upright, he ground out, "Shannon. Listen to me. Ferrare's men are scanning the building. They're using infrared sensors. That means they're looking through the walls and counting the warm bodies in each apartment."

She slapped his ear with her open hand this time, and the

reverberation of pain made his entire head hurt, but to grab her free hand, he would have to let go of her mouth.

He continued grimly, "They know you live alone. If they see two people in your apartment, they'll come investigate. Swear to God, I'm not attacking you. I'm trying to give them only one heat signature to see in here. But the way you're thrashing around, they're either going to think you're having a seizure or two people are having wild monkey sex in here. Either way," he finished, "they'll come investigate."

She finally went still beneath him.

Thank God.

She tried to speak beneath his hand. Keeping a hold of her other hand, he pushed up against her wrist enough to look down at her. Although her gaze was still wild, he thought he saw reason in its depths.

"If you scream," he murmured, "the neighbors will hear. They'll call the police, and then one of two things will happen. Police officers Ferrare has bought off will respond to the call and kill us when they find my equipment. Or I'll be arrested and hauled out of here. I'll get released from jail in a day or two, when my superiors sort out the mess with the Gavronese government, and in the meantime, Ferrare's informants at the police department will tell him you helped an American soldier spy on him and his men will come over here and kill you. But either way, you end up dead. Do you understand me?"

Her eyes went even bigger and darker than they already were, but she nodded beneath his hand.

"If I take my hand away, will you keep quiet?"

Another nod.

He lifted his hand away from her mouth. He held his breath for several seconds, but she made no sound.

He said quietly, "I'm sorry I scared you. But I swear I won't hurt you." He added wryly, "And based on the violence of your reaction just now, apparently I also need to swear I won't ever make any sexual advances toward you."

She absorbed that in silence, thinking long enough for him to register dainty curves and entirely feminine softness against his body. Were she not nearly out of her mind with fear, he'd probably have reacted like a starving man at a feast. But as it was, his groin was still throbbing from her knee shot, and terrified women were a distinct turn-off to him.

"How long do you have to lie on top of me?" she mumbled.

He sighed. "Another minute or two ought to do it."

Silence fell between them. It grew awkward. So, what did a guy talk about with a woman, anyway, while lying on top of her in a wildly suggestive pose, to distract her from said pose?

Shannon finally broke the silence. She asked in a small voice, "So. Do you do this kind of thing often?"

"What? Jump on a woman in her bed and scare her to death?" He snorted. "Not so much."

"No. This hiding from infrared scanners thing."

He shrugged. "Most of the time my targets don't know to look for me, so I don't have to dodge this sort of high-tech countersurveillance."

Silence fell again, but after a few moments Shannon commented with audible disgust, "I want my money back from my self-defense instructor. That's twice now you've attacked me and subdued me without the slightest problem."

He replied, "I wouldn't say I had no problems. You got a couple good shots in on me, there."

"But not enough to stop you."

"True. Most self-defense classes teach you how to drive off a casual attacker. Someone who'll leave and move on to an easier target if you demonstrate preparedness to make his job difficult. It's a whole different game to fend off or take down someone who's seriously motivated to subdue or kill you. You have to be prepared to take serious damage yourself. And for what it's worth, your self-defense instructor probably couldn't beat me in a fight, either, so don't feel too bad. If you'd like, I can show you a few moves out of the professional's playbook sometime."

She stared up at him. "Why would you do that?"

He frowned. "So you can feel safe."

"I'd rather *be* safe."

"In the interest of full disclosure, I have to respond that true safety is an illusion. Nobody's ever safe."

She blinked up at him, clearly appalled. "How's that?"

"We're all subject to accidents, acts of nature, illnesses beyond our control. To being in the wrong place at the wrong time."

She shrugged beneath him. "Of course nobody can control stuff like that. But there's a lot a person can do to protect themselves from being the victim of a crime. To keep someone from killing them."

He snorted at that one. "Honey, there's not a person on this planet I couldn't kill if I set my mind to it. Short of retreating to a very deep cave and having someone you utterly trust bring you food and water for the rest of your life, there's no such thing as hiding from a man like me..."

...and maybe he shouldn't have said that.

Shannon had gone completely still beneath him again, and every last vestige of color had drained from her face. She was nearly as white as the sheets she lay on.

She whispered in a choked voice, "When will we know if they've spotted you?"

A knock sounded on her hallway door, and both of their heads jerked up, startled, at the noise.

He looked down at her grimly. "They spotted me."

Chapter 5

Shannon's adrenaline spiked yet again, sending her pulse skyrocketing. She whispered frantically, "Oh, God. What do I do?"

Jake rolled off her fast, murmuring low, "Go answer the door. I'll hide in here and cover you. If anyone tries to hurt you, I swear I'll rescue you."

She stared at him in dismay. She was no good at lying, let alone hiding panic. This was never going to work. But his words of a moment ago still resonated through her brain. They'd kill her if they caught her helping him.

Jake gave her a little shove. "Yell out that you're coming. Go!"

Robotlike, she rolled off her bed. "Coming!" she called. *Oh, God. Oh, God.*

She headed for the front door with Jake on her heels. Her fingers fumbled terribly with the chain as he snapped up his duffel bags and sprinted for the bedroom. With a quick glance over her shoulder to make sure he was out of sight, she somehow managed to get the lock unlatched. Jake would protect her. This would be okay. She could do this. Do it or die. *Oh, God.*

The door swung open. For a moment, she stared uncomprehending at the familiar and smiling face of her neighbor from across the hall, the ever-nosy Octavius.

"Hello, darling!" the big man gushed as he pushed past her into her living room. "How have you been? I haven't seen you for days. I was beginning to suspect you'd thrown me over for some delicious hunk of a man you're hiding from me. I just had to bring you some of these roses I found down at the market. Ten dollars U.S. for two dozen of them, can you believe it?"

The man did, indeed, have a big armload of bloodred roses, and their perfume was thick and heady in Shannon's nose. She trailed her neighbor as he barged into her kitchen. He turned and stared expectantly at her. When she did nothing, he sang out, "Hellooo. Vase, please."

"Oh. Uhh, yeah." She opened her pantry and fished out a vase large enough to hold the long-stemmed roses.

"New laptop?" her neighbor asked as he commenced efficiently stripping leaves off the lower stems of the flowers.

She glanced at the dining table in alarm. Thank God the top was down and Jake's surveillance shots weren't visible. "Uhh, yeah. New laptop."

"Did I wake you up or something?" Octavius threw over his shoulder. "You're acting like a zombie."

Nap. Perfect. "Yes, you did wake me up. I lay down for a little siesta."

He turned to look at her. "Since when? Two things you never do—naps and men."

She thought about the man in her bedroom at this very

moment, no doubt overhearing that remark, and her cheeks heated up. She protested, "I do, too, do naps!"

Octavius laughed. "We have *got* to get you a man, girlfriend. You're getting cranky in your old age. There's this aerobics instructor down at my gym—let me fix you up with him."

She looked at the man's soft, three-hundred-pound frame. "You go to a gym?" she asked in disbelief.

"Not to work out, of course," Octavius replied indignantly. "I can't stand to sweat. But the view of all those glistening, muscular, half-naked bodies…" He fanned himself. "It's better than a strip club. You really ought to come with me sometime. Check out the local talent."

Shannon grimaced. "We've been over all this before. I'm not into men, okay?"

Octavius shrugged. "Fine. You watch the girls and I'll watch the boys."

She laughed helplessly. "You're incorrigible."

"That's me, baby." Octavius moved out of the kitchen and back to the living room. "I love what you've done with the place."

Shannon glanced around, startled. "What are you talking—" She broke off. Jake had moved the armoire off the side wall and diagonally into the corner. Probably to hide all the wires and doodads running to all of his equipment inside it. "Oh. You're always telling me that change is good. I decided to take your advice."

Before she could say or do a thing to stop him, Octavius moved over to her bedroom door and flung it open. Shannon gasped. She started to lurch forward, visions of her neighbor with a giant dent in the back of his skull dancing through her mind's eye.

"Have you made any changes in here?" her rapidly growing annoyingly nosy visitor called out.

"No!" She followed him into her bedroom. Oh, Lord. How

was she supposed to explain Jake's presence? Octavius had heard her declare over and over that she hated men and wanted nothing to do with them. She could claim he was her brother. Except she must have mentioned to Octavius sometime over the past few years that she had no brothers or sisters. A cousin, then.

"Oooh! What's in these bags?"

Octavius's exclamation drew her gaze sharply to Jake's two large duffel bags sitting in the corner of her room. *Oh, crap.* She looked around the room fast. No sign of Jake. He'd apparently managed to find a place to hide but hadn't had time to stash his gear.

"Uhh, that's scuba gear. I thought I'd take it up. You're always telling me to get out of the house. To do something new. I hear there's good diving off the Gavronese coast."

Octavius waved an uninterested hand. "There are reefs or something."

"So. If you're done inspecting my apartment, will you help me arrange the roses? You know I suck at that sort of thing."

"It's not that hard. You just need to put a few marbles in the bottom of the vase to prop up the stems. Then start with the middle flowers and work your way outward…." Thankfully, her tactic worked. He headed for the kitchen and the flowers lying on her counter. Shannon gave one last look around her bedroom but spotted no sign of Jake. He must be in the bathroom, or maybe her closet. She breathed a sigh of relief and stepped out into the living room, closing the door quietly behind her.

She thought she'd successfully gotten Octavius off the subject of men, but apparently not. As he efficiently trimmed and arranged her roses into a stunning display of crimson, he asked, "You sure you're not holding out on me? You'd tell me if you got yourself a man, wouldn't you?"

Alarm bells clanged wildly in her gut. Why would he push her on the subject of a man unless someone had told him to come into her place and find out who was with her? Jake's earlier words about Octavius being a possible informant for the criminal living across the street flashed through her head.

She answered as casually as she could muster. "Of course I wouldn't tell you. Two minutes after I did, all of Gavarone would know."

"Aww, c'mon, Shan. I can keep a secret."

She laughed. "Yeah, but that doesn't mean you ever do."

Octavius laughed back. "Bitch."

"You admit, then, that I'm right."

"Of course." He stepped back from the roses to admire his work. "There. Perfect. Now, put these on your coffee table where they'll scent your entire apartment. And by the way, I cast a voodoo spell on them. So look out."

Octavius was originally from Jamaica and she didn't put it past him to know a voodoo spell or two. "And just what kind of spell was it?" she demanded.

"A love spell. Gonna conjure you up a man. A good-looking, sexy one who'll make you remember what it's like to be a real woman."

"I'm a real woman," she protested.

"When's the last time you had sex?"

"That's none of your business!" Shannon exclaimed. She felt compelled to add, "But I'm no nun."

"Playing with battery-operated toys ain't real sex, sweetie. I'm talking about sweaty, grunting, headboard-banging, screaming-orgasm sex."

Shannon's jaw sagged. How in the heck was she supposed to answer that? Particularly with Jake hiding somewhere in the next room listening to every word of this?

"You smell those flowers three times a day, a big deep whiff of 'em. And sure as I'm standing here, a man's gonna come your way." And with that pronouncement, Octavius breezed out of the apartment.

Shannon stared at the closed door behind him.

"He always like that?" a male voice murmured low from behind her.

"Pretty much." She headed for the front door to lock it and put the chain back in place.

"Force of nature, that guy." Jake was rooting through the roses as if he'd lost something among them.

"You have no idea." She turned to face Jake. "What are you doing?" she blurted.

"Checking for bugs."

Man, talk about paranoid. She shook her head. And then she sighed. Might as well get it over with. Her face felt as if it was going to catch fire any second. But thankfully, Jake made no comment about Octavius's wildly inappropriate comments about men and her sex life—or lack thereof.

"Sorry about the bags. I had no time to hide them before your friend came into the bedroom to hunt for me. Good thinking on the scuba-gear thing. Of course, now you're actually going to have to take up scuba diving. Or at least take a few lessons."

"He was hunting for you?"

"Of course. Why else would your neighbor barge into your home and into your bedroom uninvited? And then there was that question asking if you were sure you didn't have a man in your life and would you tell him. Oh, yeah. He was sent in here to spot me."

"But he didn't find anyone. So we're okay, right?" she asked hopefully. Her gut already knew the answer to the question, but she could hope, at any rate.

Jake didn't bother to answer her. He just gave her a "you know better than that" look. And he was right.

"Now what?" she asked quietly.

He sighed. "As much as I was hoping to hunker down here and be invisible until my mission's over, we're going to have to come up with a cover story and go public."

"Go public? What does that mean?"

Again he didn't answer her question directly. "Do you have any brothers or male cousins between the ages of thirty and forty?"

"Nope. No siblings, and my uncle and his wife have only three daughters."

He cursed under his breath. "I guess that leaves us no choice, then."

When he didn't continue, she asked hesitantly, "No choice about what?"

"I'm going to have to be the boyfriend."

"No!" The word was out of her mouth before she had time to think about it.

He looked at her quizzically. "Why not?"

She really, really didn't want to go there. She took a deep breath and answered resolutely. "You heard me with Octavius. I don't do men."

"I thought you told him you're not interested in girls, either."

"I don't do sex. Relationships. None of that stuff."

His gaze was intent. Focused. Undoubtedly catching and analyzing every nuance of her expression. "Why not?"

She shrugged. "I just don't."

He sighed. "I'm afraid I have to know why. We've got to build a cover story that'll hold up to scrutiny, and we don't have much time to do it. If you won't help me, I'll have my headquarters dig up every detail of your life and come up with something that will work."

He might as well have stabbed her in the gut with a knife. A big, sharp one. She sat down heavily on the sofa. He sat gingerly beside her, but far enough away that she didn't feel threatened. *Huh. Progress.* Two hours ago, she'd have panicked if he sat that close to her. "This isn't fair, Jake. I didn't ask you to invade my life and take over my home, and now you want me to lay out all the most private details of my past for you? I don't even *know* you."

Something resembling compassion glinted in his eyes for a moment before they went cold and hard, impersonal, again. He answered quietly, "You're absolutely correct. I have no right to ask this of you. But I'm asking anyway. Please help me. This mission is important."

"Why? Who is this Ferrare guy?"

"He's the one who got away."

"I beg your pardon?"

"A few years back, he was one of the largest and most ruthless drug dealers in this part of the world. My teammates and I chased him and his empire for two years before we finally took him down. We thought we'd killed him. Hell, we were sure we'd killed him. And then a few weeks ago, he surfaced again. It's like the guy rose from the dead. This man nearly killed just about everyone on my team at one time or another. He's deadlier than any snake. And he's back. I've got to stop him before he rebuilds his empire. Before he goes after his daughters and tries to kill them. Hell, before he comes after my teammates looking for revenge."

She didn't know where to start responding to that speech. Okay. So the guy was violent and dangerous. He'd even try to kill his own daughters? Wow. Make that really violent. "So this is a personal vendetta for you, then."

"No!" Jake replied sharply. "I just...never fail. I had this guy in my sights. I watched him die in the arms of my best friend. He was *dead*. Mission accomplished."

"And now he's back."

"Right."

"So this is about professional pride, then?" she asked.

Jake frowned at her. Apparently, it wasn't nearly that simple, either.

"What's so important about this guy that I'm supposed to strip my life bare for you?" she pressed.

Jake closed his eyes. He didn't look like he was going to answer. But then he opened them, his silver gaze pinning her to her seat. "I had a premonition a long time ago that Eduardo Ferrare was going to kill me. From the very first time I got a mission brief about him, I knew. He was the one. He would end it all for me. When he died, I was so relieved I could hardly believe it. My gut had been wrong. I had outlived him. I dodged Fate. And then a few weeks ago, I get this call. I get handed a stack of pictures, and I'm told he's been spotted in Gavarone." He shrugged. "And here I am. Trying to cheat Death a second time."

"You believe in all that destiny stuff?" she asked, surprised. He seemed like such a pragmatist. So very much a believer in the idea of being able to control every aspect of his life. "I wouldn't have guessed it of you."

"Of all people, I have to believe that we each have an appointed time to die. The choices people make lead to logical consequences, and one of those is death. They die when they're supposed to."

Understanding exploded across her brain, along with such shock that she merely sat there and stared at him. This man wasn't a spy. He was an *assassin*.

"You don't watch people for a living. You *kill* them for a living," she accused. When he didn't say anything, she demanded, "Don't you?"

He sighed. It was a gentle sound. A light breeze rustling through green leaves. A breath of spring warming a cool morning. "Yes, Shannon. That's what I do. I kill people."

She stared, her brain completely unable, or perhaps unwilling, to form some sort of response to that.

"Aren't you going to ask me the next logical question?" he murmured.

"Huh?" Words still weren't coming to her. Heck, rational thought seemed beyond her at the moment.

"Ask me if I'm planning to kill you."

She blinked once. Twice. This must be what it felt like when time stopped. It was as if she were in a bubble, a private world all her own, where nothing moved or changed. Where time and space had no meaning. How long she stayed in that place of suspended animation, she had no idea. But finally, a single thought formed. It made its way to her mouth, and she opened her lips. To her surprise, actual sound came forth.

"Are you? Are you planning to kill me?"

Chapter 6

Jake held his breath, watching as she absorbed his revelation. She was such a creature of nervous motion that he fully expected her to leap up and run away screaming. But surprisingly, she just sat there. Still. Frozen. It was as if her brain refused to compute what he'd just said.

When she finally spoke, to ask him if he planned to kill her, her voice was calm. Too calm. She must be in some sort of minor shock.

"No, Shannon. I am not planning to kill you. In fact, I'm planning to do everything in my power to keep you safe and to make sure you come to no harm because of helping me."

"And everything in your power is rather considerable, I gather."

An image of a giant underground bunker filled with high-tech gear, satellite links and special operators flashed through his head. He replied dryly, "Rather."

"So you really can find out everything there is to know about me?"

He sighed. "As we speak, my colleagues are in touch with the United States Attorney General's office to get your legal records unsealed. They'll have access by tomorrow morning."

That finally launched her into motion. She jumped up, her hands jerking in agitation. She moved across the room to her bookshelf and straightened a figurine. She ran a finger across the shelf and wiped the nonexistent dust from it on her pant leg. Across the room to tweak the drapes. Back to the other side of the room to adjust the angle of her phone on the counter, and then off to the armchair to fluff the pillow sitting on it.

He waited patiently for the explosion to come. But thankfully, it wasn't nearly as spectacular as he expected. "Why are you doing this to me?" she demanded.

"It's nothing personal. You happen to live in the right apartment to look down on Ferrare, and you happen to be American. Random circumstance, if you will."

The color drained from her face abruptly. He thought he detected a slight sway as she stood there, frozen, staring unseeing at him. Her voice waxed distant, disconnected, as she spoke. "That's what they said about Lucifer, too."

"Lucifer?" What did the devil have to do with this? Was she making some obscure biblical reference he wasn't catching?

"Lucifer Jones. He's the man who climbed in my bedroom window and nearly killed me a few years back. It was nothing personal, they said. He just liked the look of my house and knew a single woman lived there."

"Is he what we're going to find in that sealed Justice Department file?"

She nodded miserably.

"Where is Jones now?"

"Prison."

"When is he due out?"

"Any day."

Jake swore again. No wonder his showing up at her door and forcing his way in had scared the bejeezus out of her. "Is Jones smart enough or connected enough to send someone else after you?"

"His brother was some kind of bigwig criminal in Chicago, connected with a gang. He and Lucifer had a bunch of drug charges against them, but none of them had ever stuck."

When gangsters were getting off at trial, it was because someone was paying for them to have a high-powered attorney. "Do you know which gang they were in? Which drug cartel they worked for?"

"I'm not sure. And in answer to your question, Lucifer wouldn't send someone else after me. He'd do the dirty work himself. Of that I *am* sure."

A sick, sadistic bastard, then. And this gentle, sweet woman had been his victim? Something hot and violent erupted in Jake's gut. *What the hell was that?* It rose up, nearly choking him, heating up his face and making his eyeballs ache. Holy crap. That was...

...rage.

Shannon stopped roaming long enough to ask, her voice dripping in irony, "Aren't you going to ask me the next logical question? 'What did he do to you, Shannon?'"

It was all Jake could do to stay seated on the couch, to force himself not to leap up and wrap her in his arms, to vow to her that he'd protect her from this monster, to vow to himself to kill the guy for her.

From behind tight jaws he managed to answer evenly, "Nothing you can say will unduly shock me. In my line of work, I've been witness to atrocities on an epic scale. I won't judge."

"You're going to find out about it anyway if you read my file. It's all in there."

She startled him by coming over to the couch and dropping down heavily upon it. She spoke emotionlessly, like she was reciting a speech by heart. "I was a schoolteacher outside of Chicago. As I've already mentioned, I lived alone. My first place. A sweet little bungalow I'd fixed up all by myself. It wasn't the kind of town where people were tense about locking their doors, but I did anyway. I was cautious. Sensible. Looked out for myself." Her voice broke a little. "I thought I was safe. Nothing bad could ever happen to me."

She paused, and Jake's arms ached to pull her against his chest. He sensed her gathering herself to continue. When she did, her voice wasn't quite so steady.

"It was like any other summer night. Cool and pleasant after a hot day. I left my window open like everyone else in town that night. He cut the screen and pulled himself through the window. He was a big man, nearly six and a half feet tall. He was quiet, though. I didn't wake up until he was on top of me. He had a knife to my throat."

Jake saw her hands clench into fists, but Shannon gave no other indication that the telling of this story affected her. She continued woodenly, "I fought. Tried to scream. But he got a hand over my mouth and slugged me in the temple. When I woke up, I was tied to my bed, gagged and naked. And sore. He'd already...done things to me. I could see him through my bedroom door, lying on my couch, eating food from my refrigerator and watching my television."

Jake detected a brittle quality to her posture, and it worried him. "You don't have to do this if you don't want to."

Shannon glared daggers at him—her first show of emotion since starting her tale. "You wanted to know. You might as well hear it all."

She spent the next fifteen minutes describing in detached,

clinical detail horrors that made Jake's skin crawl. He'd undoubtedly seen worse in his day, but he'd never personally known the victims of torture and assault. And that made all the difference.

Eventually, blessedly, Shannon fell silent. She sat, still and unmoving. If he didn't know better, he'd say the recitation hadn't affected her at all. But her knuckles were stark white where her fists clenched together, and that awful fragile quality still clung to her.

Cautiously, he asked, "How did you get away from him?"

"He got careless. He'd untied me to take me to the restroom, and he didn't tie my wrists quite tight enough when he redid it. I was able to pull one hand free—dislocated my thumb, but it was worth it. Then I untied my other bonds. I crawled out the same window he'd come in and ran next door. I don't know who was more shocked. My neighbor at finding a naked woman at his door in the middle of the night or me for actually getting away alive."

Jake finished the story for her, his voice hoarse even to his ears. "Then you testified and the jury convicted him. You moved down here and left behind everything and everyone. And you started a new life."

She nodded, staring down at her hands. A single tear fell, splashing onto the back of her hand. And he broke.

"May I touch you?" he rasped.

She looked up, surprised.

"I want to hug you, but I don't know if you'll let me."

That made her frown. Nope. Not going to let him share her private hell. Damn. He didn't know which he needed worse—to comfort her or to smash his fist through something.

And then the darnedest thing happened. She slid across the couch. She didn't look up at him, but she inched closer until her knee touched his, and then her thigh, and then her whole side. And then she leaned into him. Her hands were still clenched fiercely in her lap, but she laid her head against his chest.

Carefully, so very carefully, he brought his arms up around her, holding her like she was made of hand-blown glass.

A sob escaped her.

They sat like that for a long time, her body rigid and his shirt slowly getting soaked as silent tears ran down her face. Hell if he knew what to do. He'd lived his whole life around men. You gave a guy a bear hug, punctuated it with a couple of fist thumps on the back, and then the bonding moment was over. But this slow-leaking emotion stuff was a mystery.

Finally, as he thought maybe he felt the tension begin to drain from her, Jake dared to murmur, "You're possibly the bravest person I've ever met."

For some reason, that threw her emotional floodgates wide open. She cried her heart out then, shaking against his chest and turning his front into Niagara Falls. And somewhere in there, he sort of got the hang of comforting her. It really boiled down to just being with her. Holding her. Rubbing her back a little with his hand. Digging out a handkerchief when the worst of it was over for her to mop her eyes. Not commenting about how her remaining mascara was heading at high speed for her chin. Actually finding the clown look endearing.

Eventually, Shannon raised her head and gave a big, unladylike sniff. "I'm so sorry. I've never fallen apart like that before when I've told the story."

And from somewhere compassionate and gentle inside him that he'd never had the slightest idea existed, he said in a deep, calm voice, "Maybe it was time to let it go."

"But you didn't bargain for that when you asked what was in my file."

He shrugged. "I asked, didn't I?"

"Not for the boo-hooing bit, though. The lawyers coached

me long and hard on how not to cry when I took the stand. They didn't want me to look like a hysterical female."

He smiled. "I wouldn't say you're hysterical. More like only mildly hilarious."

"Ha-ha." A tiny smile cracked her face, and he breathed a huge sigh of relief. The crisis had passed.

"If you don't mind talking about it just a little bit more, what was he sentenced to?" he asked.

"Twenty-five to life. Eligible for parole in ten years. Less for good behavior."

Uh-oh. She was back to robotspeak. He frowned. "How does a bastard like that rate parole? He nearly killed you."

"His lawyer argued that Lucifer never actually tried to kill me, so they couldn't convict him of attempted murder. They only got him on an assortment of aggravated assault, torture and sexual-assault charges."

"But he told you he planned to kill you when he was done—"

She interrupted, a distinct note of bitterness tingeing her words. "Ahh, but he denied saying it. His word against mine. His lawyer said that I was under extreme duress at the time, and my memory was suspect. Since I didn't stick around as his prisoner long enough for him to actually kill me or at least try, he got the parole option."

He'd promised not to judge. Just to listen. But it was nigh unto impossible for Jake not to rail against a system that would let a monster like that out of jail. Ever. Jones needed to be locked up and the key thrown away.

Jake realized his entire body was tense. Iron hard. And Shannon looked like she was starting to pick up on it. Her hands were beginning to flutter in her lap like helpless, injured sparrows.

He laid his hands on top of hers. "I'm here now. Lucifer Jones isn't going to get within a mile of you. I'll kill him first.

Do you hear me? He's not getting anywhere near you. Not on my watch."

The wounded birds stilled for the moment.

"You're under orders to sleep well at night and not worry when you're awake. This is what I do for a living. I track down and wipe out men like him."

She frowned. "But you're here to go after someone else. I don't want to distract you from your real job."

"You're part of the job. I'm supposed to protect my cover. If Lucifer Jones gets anywhere near you, he's a dead man."

She studied him for a long time. Finally, she gave him a single, small nod. She stood up and resumed fussing where she'd left off before.

"Why are you still tense, Shannon? Is there something else you're not telling me?"

That made her smile a little. "I'm just feeling a little... naked. I've bared my soul to you, and yet I know practically nothing about you. It feels lopsided."

He supposed he knew what she was talking about. "What do you suggest we do to correct that?"

She glanced up at him, capturing his gaze for just a moment before hers slid away. "I suppose you could tell me something private and personal about yourself."

That made him jerk back. Hard. Private and personal? He didn't do that with anyone. Not even his teammates with whom he'd spent years and thought of as brothers. "How private and personal are we talking here?"

She shrugged. "I don't know your innermost secrets, so I can't really answer that. I'll have to trust your judgment on it. How did you become an assassin?"

"I'm not an assassin. I'm a sniper."

"What's the difference?"

"One's civilian, maybe or maybe not working for the good guys, maybe on salary, maybe working on contracts. Snipers are government, or in my case, military. Doing sanctioned military missions."

"You haven't answered the question. How did you become a killer?"

He flinched at that. Hard to believe that in the eyes of some, he was a worse criminal than Lucifer Jones. "It started with my father. He was a Vietnam vet. Specialized in finding trip wires and clearing tunnels. He was messed up bad in the head. Married a whacked-out drug addict, and they had me. Mom fried her brains too bad to care for me, and crazy Dad was stuck with the kid. He took me to live with him in the woods. We'd go out for a month at a time with a parachute, a handful of matches and a knife, and live off the land."

The memories flowed over him, surprisingly vivid in his mind given how long it had been since he'd allowed himself to think about that time in his life. He continued.

"Some people say I was raised more like an animal than a human being. I got good at sneaking up on wildlife. At being still and quiet. At not thinking much about death. It was me hungry or the animal dead."

She came back to the couch to sit beside him. Not in touching range, but close enough to feel her body heat. "How did you end up in the military yourself if it messed up your dad so bad?"

Jake sighed. Okay, so now they were getting plenty private and personal. He was about to reveal something he'd never told a single one of his teammates. Setting aside the old humiliation, he plowed on. "My dad liked to drink. He stole a fifth of grain alcohol from a liquor store, got stinking drunk on top of his usual depression and ended up hanging himself. I found him. I cut him down and buried him in the woods."

He started as her soft, warm hand closed over his and give it an encouraging squeeze.

"Thing was, the owner of the liquor store had a surveillance camera and filmed a filthy, bearded mountain man about my height and weight stealing the booze. The sheriff came looking for us and found me. I fit the general description of my old man, and the sheriff arrested me. The justice of the peace knew my dad had been in 'Nam and was a head case. He cut me a break. Gave me a choice. Join the army or go to jail. My dad was dead. I was seventeen. Barely literate. Antisocial. And the only thing in the whole world I knew how to do was hunt. I chose the army."

"You don't look or sound much like that kid."

"A little structure in a person's life is a wondrous thing. With the help of a few hard-nosed drill instructors who, at the end of the day, genuinely gave a damn about me, I got my act together. I availed myself of the G.I. Bill to get an education and applied to sniper school as soon as I was eligible. The rest, as they say, is history."

"Do you like what you do?"

The question jolted him. "It isn't something you like. It's something you do because it's necessary. Like a surgeon cutting off a person's mangled leg. It's not pleasant, but someone has to do it."

"Why you?"

"Why not me? I'm very, very good at it. And I serve my country."

She startled him by reaching out with both hands and placing them on each of his cheeks. She gazed deeply into his eyes, her own expression turbulent. Intense. "Yes, Jake. But at what cost?"

He stared, uncomprehending.

She repeated in a whisper, "At what cost?"

Chapter 7

Shannon stared at Jake, watching the subtle play of emotions across his face. Slowly, she was learning to read him. It took close attention and a good eye for detail, but the signs were there. And at the moment, he had no intention of answering her question. He was choosing to pretend it was rhetorical. Which, in fact, it was not.

Jake Harrington was a decent man. A good man, even. She was absolutely convinced of that. And if she was right, someone like him couldn't possibly make a career out of killing people without it taking some terrible toll on his psyche. If she was wrong… Well, then Jake Harrington was a worse monster than Lucifer Jones had ever dreamed of being.

And there was no way that was true. None.

Of course, it wasn't like she could cast stones at the guy for avoiding facing hard questions. Lord knew, she'd been at it for years.

She'd spent a long time wondering if Jones had any regrets

about what he'd done to her. If he felt remorse. Or if he was simply very pissed that she got away from him and that he got caught. She figured it came down to whether or not the guy had a soul. If he did, his deeds would surely catch up with him someday. If not, she wished him well in the deepest, darkest depths of Hell.

What about Jake? Did he have a soul? How could he not? He couldn't have empathized with her enough to comfort her and share her pain if he didn't have one.

Jake interrupted her reverie, which surprised her. So far he hadn't been the type to initiate conversation. "We still have to figure out how to explain you suddenly getting a boyfriend. The story will have to hold up to close scrutiny from Ferrare's people. It's going to be seen as way out of character for you to hook up with me."

She snorted. No kidding. Not only was he a man; he was a dangerous, predatory sort of man. Octavius was going to sprout feathers and lay an egg when he met Jake.

"What's so funny?" Jake asked.

"I was thinking about how Octavius is going to react when he meets you. He'll have a stroke."

Jake grinned. "I suspect I may react about the same way to him."

A giggle escaped her at the notion. "Well, it's sure going to surprise him."

Jake looked thoughtful. "That may be it. A surprise. You and I have known each other for some time in some other venue. And I surprised you by dropping in to visit. My work brought me to town, and I took the opportunity to meet in person. Do you ever do anything over the Internet? Chat rooms? Interest groups? Loops of friends?"

"I tutor kids over the Internet to supplement my income. If you think teaching pays bad in the States, you ought to see what teachers make down here."

"Perfect. You and I met on the Internet. We've been chat buddies for years. I've come to town, looking to take it to the next level."

"You think your criminal guy will buy that?"

"It's plausible. My headquarters can make up and plant a chat history between the two of us on the Internet."

She frowned. "But what about the time-date groups on the transmissions?"

"Kid stuff to the people I work with."

Wow. "What do you do for a fake living, fake Mr. Harrington?"

He thought for a minute. "I'm a life coach. I act as a personal trainer, nutrition consultant, motivational speaker and guru. You and I hooked up because you're trying to put your life back together."

She laughed. "Guru Jake. Master of alfalfa sprouts and yoga. Yup, it's you all the way."

His eyes sparkled with humor, and the effect on his face was stunning. For a moment, the serious, introverted professional looked almost…happy. Boyish. Charming. And had that actually been a hint of a dimple she'd spied? Perish the thought! Determination to make him laugh and see if he really did have dimples suffused her.

"So, Shannon. Are you ready to go out in public and be seen with me?"

"I guess so. Where are we going?"

"I need to buy some plants to put in the flowerpots," he replied. "And the sooner Ferrare's men see us together, the better. When Octavius reports back that he didn't find a man in your apartment, it's going to send up all kinds of red flags with Ferrare's security people."

She glanced over at the row of brightly painted ceramic pots. "Did I mention that I kill every plant I come within ten feet of? Two weeks, tops, and your flowers will be dead as a doornail."

"You're in luck. I'm good with growing stuff."

She headed for the kitchen counter and her purse. She threw over her shoulder, "Who'd have guessed? A killer botanist?"

When she met him at the front door, he paused with his hand on the knob. "You and I are still getting to know one another. There's no need to hold hands or act romantic."

"Can I check out your butt when you're not looking?"

His gaze snapped to hers. That was definitely shock in his gaze for a moment. "Uhh, sure. Mind if I do the same?"

Okay, so that idea made her blush. "Just don't let me catch you. I'd hate to have to slap you in public."

An actual grin flickered at the corners of his mouth. Not quite enough to pop the alleged dimples, but close. Drat. He opened the door and stepped through first, ushering her out only after he'd given the hallway a quick look.

It turned out to be surprisingly easy. They rode the elevator down to the lobby, walked out onto the street across from the Ferrare compound and strolled past the tall stucco wall and down the block to a small outdoor market. Jake gazed around casually, for all the world a tourist out enjoying the sights. It was hard *not* to relax in his presence, in fact. He either had nerves of steel or was a great actor. Or both.

He was examining a crate of apples beside her when she heard a faint ring tone from inside her purse. She fished out her cell phone. The caller ID said U.S. Gov't. *Crystal Wilson.* She'd completely forgotten about the woman.

"Hey, Crystal."

"Hello, Shannon. I'm sorry it took me so long to get back to you. But I've got some news for you."

Alarm erupted in her gut. "Uhh, okay. Lay it on me."

Jake looked away from the apples to her, concern glinting in his gaze. She smiled weakly at him.

"The guy you met, Jake Harrington, is definitely an employee of the U.S. government. But beyond that, I can't find out a blessed thing about him. It's as if he doesn't exist, except for just a name. I can't even tell you if he's in the military or works for some other agency. It's the darnedest thing."

"Is that the bad news or the worse news?"

"Just the bad part."

She supposed she shouldn't be surprised that Jake's identity was buried very deeply. What he did probably necessitated that. After all, he must have a boatload of enemies and people who'd like to see him dead. "Tell me the rest," she said cautiously.

"Lucifer Jones was released from prison yesterday. We put a team on him to trail him for a while. To make sure he didn't try to come after you or make contact with you."

Her stomach dropped to her feet.

"Our team lost him. He intentionally eluded them."

Shannon's mind went completely blank. It was as if a thick fog had suddenly enveloped her. Sounds and colors were muted, distant. She was all alone in this place, frozen and disconnected from reality.

"You okay?" Jake murmured.

"You okay?" Crystal asked.

"I dunno," she forced herself to mumble to both of them.

Crystal spoke in her ear. "He could be anywhere. But we got a lead on his brother. Looks like he headed for South America a few months ago. I've contacted the Gavronese Customs people to see if they got a hit on the brother, but I haven't heard back from them yet. Bottom line—you need to lay low for a while. Be careful."

Jake's hand came up to touch her elbow. "Did something happen? Somebody die?" he murmured more urgently.

"Right. Thanks." She ended the call, a humorless, faintly hysterical laugh bubbling up in her chest. A monster was on the loose, likely coming for her, and all the government could say was a lame "Be careful."

Jake leaned closed and muttered sharply in her ear. "Talk to me. What's going on?"

"Lucifer's out of jail. And he ditched the federal agents who were trailing him."

"Oh." Jake visibly relaxed.

She pivoted to face him. "Oh? That's all you have to say?"

He shrugged. "He's an amateur. I can take a guy like him out in my sleep."

"Yeah, well, he's probably here with his brother."

"Okay, so two amateurs. No problem."

She didn't know whether to be outraged or relieved. Finally she settled on echoing, "Amateurs? They're *thugs*."

He grinned. A full-blown, smug male grin. And sure enough he had the sexiest pair of dimples Shannon had seen in a long time. Too bad she didn't give a damn at the moment. "How can you be so casual? Lucifer nearly killed me!"

"I'm trained to handle stuff the Jones brothers have never dreamed of trying, honey."

He might be right, but she was still appalled at his cavalier attitude. "So, you're not in the least bit worried that they might show up here and try to finish what Lucifer started with me."

The grin disappeared. "I sincerely hope they do."

That dropped her jaw.

"Lucifer's a dead man if he tries it."

The ice in Jake's voice rocked her back on her heels. Stunned, she turned and stared blindly at crates of produce. She was startled, though, when Jake pulled out his cell phone. He murmured, "Hey, it's me. I need a high-quality photograph, preferably a bunch of them, of a man named Lucifer Jones. Released from federal prison in the past day or two. And his brother, if you can find some. The brother's a small-time thug from the Chicago area. Yeah, ASAP. Thanks."

He took her arm in his gentle but unbreakable grasp and steered her to a fishmonger's stand. "You up for some of that jellied squid?" he asked lightly.

The suggestion startled her into laughing. "Not in a million years."

"Thank God," he murmured.

She looked all around, half turning to glance carefully behind them, as well.

"You need to stop that," Jake murmured without taking his eyes off an array of fish fillets on ice.

"Why? My self-defense teacher said it's important to be aware of everything and everyone around you."

"It's equally important not to convey a sense of fear and insecurity to would-be attackers. Besides, I already know we're being tailed."

She lurched, slamming into him in her panic. His arm went around her, and he fetched her up hard against him. "Easy, there. You okay?"

"No, Jake Harrington, I'm damn well not okay," she bit out.

He smiled winningly down at her. "It's not the Jones boys behind us. It's one of Ferrare's thugs."

"Oh." The tension drained out of her body all at once.

One corner of his mouth turned down sardonically. "I wouldn't get that comfortable if I were you. My thug is likely a hell of a lot more dangerous than your thug."

"What do we do now?"

"Same thing we were already doing. A little shopping, a little sightseeing, a little getting to know each other."

Right. No sweat.

He dragged her over to an incense vendor. "What's your favorite scent?"

She stared at the sticks. "Sandalwood, I guess."

"Me, too. I also like the pine-scented stuff."

"Do you like floral scents?" she asked him.

He shrugged. "I don't get much opportunity to smell girly stuff. The guys I work with aren't about to light up a vanilla-rose candle and sit in a bubble bath."

She grinned at him. "They don't know what they're missing." She bought a couple of candles, one lavender scented, and the other a purely girly gardenia candle.

The market wound a couple of blocks into the old town district of St. George, where the streets were narrow and twisting. They rounded one such corner when, from behind them, a male voice spoke in menacing English. "Step into the alley. Don't make a fuss or I'll kill you both."

Her first reaction was profound relief that the voice wasn't Lucifer's. Her second reaction was further relief that Jake was with her. Her third reaction was curiosity as to how he was going to handle this. And only belatedly did it occur to her that she probably ought to be scared out of her mind.

Jake steered her off the main street and into a dark little alley just to their right. He maneuvered her behind him and then backed up, forcing her deeper into the cul-de-sac. His voice was shockingly calm as he told the man who'd followed them, "You know, it's not nice to threaten a lady."

"Shut up, Americano."

A definite note of chill crept into Jake's voice. "Is there something you'd like to say to me?"

"Yeah. Hand over your wallet and your watch and the lady's purse. I've got a knife, and I know how to use it."

"That's too bad," Jake murmured pleasantly.

"Huh?" The mugger sounded surprised. She wished she could see more over Jake's shoulder, but she couldn't make out much in the gloom anyway. Jake's entire body had gone relaxed. Ready. Waiting. That predatory thing she'd initially feared in him was rolling off his back in thick waves.

"If you hadn't mentioned a weapon, I would have just neutralized you and walked away. But now that you've threatened a lady with a knife, I'm going to have to beat the crap out of you."

The mugger leaped.

Shannon screamed and stumbled back as Jake exploded into motion. It was over so fast she didn't really see what he did. But before she knew it, Jake had the guy on the ground. The knife clattered away into the shadows, and Jake began methodically pounding the guy's face into pulp.

His facial expression never varied. He was focused, to be sure, but showed absolutely no reaction to the blood spraying him, showed no interest in the guy's screams and then whimpers for mercy. Only cold efficiency emanated from him.

This was a true killer.

Lucifer Jones was mentally unstable. Acting out anger and violent impulses. Lacking in morals or social conscience. But he was absolutely nothing like the calm, cool killer dismantling the man on the ground before her.

"Jake!" she cried. "Stop! You're killing him!"

He glanced up at her, his eyes colorless. Emotionless. "No, I'm not. If I wanted to kill him, he'd have been dead the first time I hit him."

How could he be so unconcerned? "What are you doing?" she whispered.

"I'm teaching him a lesson."

"I think he's learned it," she ventured. She had to calm Jake down. Although if he got much calmer, he might doze off. She had to break him out of whatever fugue state he'd dropped into. Although in all fairness to Jake, the other guy had attacked first.

Jake glanced down at the battered and bleeding mess curled up at his feet. Glanced back up at her. Then he leaned down and whispered something in the guy's ear too quietly for her to hear. The guy nodded. Jake stepped back and watched dispassionately as the man pushed painfully to his hands and knees, panting. Blood poured from the guy's nose and mouth, and Shannon's stomach threatened to empty itself.

The man spit out a couple of white things—teeth. She *was* going to throw up now. She reached a hand out to the wall beside her to steady herself. Groaning, the man pushed himself to his feet.

"Don't forget what I said," Jake warned.

The man cast a terrified glance at Jake and then turned and stumbled toward the mouth of the alley. He broke into a stumbling run and disappeared around the corner.

Jake shook his head. "Amateur," he muttered in disgust.

She swore under her breath. No wonder he thought Lucifer was an amateur. Jake was a one-man wrecking machine! "What did you say to that guy?" Shannon murmured thickly.

Jake took a concerned step toward her. "You don't look so good. You feeling all right, honey?"

She took a sharp step back from him and whispered, "Who are you?"

Chapter 8

Jake stopped in his tracks. Clearly the lady didn't want to be touched at the moment. Christ. Did she have to see that? Talk about wrecking any semblance of trust they might have built up between them. Even a strong, confident person would quail before the display of violence he'd just unleashed. But fragile, innocent Shannon? He'd probably scarred her for life.

Jake cursed under his breath. The last thing he wanted to do was to pile more psychic wounds on top of the ones this lady already had. But he frankly didn't have time right now to pick apart her noggin or let her pick apart his. He needed to get them away from this dead-end alley before Ferrare's thug decided to come back with a few of his friends. And submachine guns. She could psychoanalyze him later.

He'd recognized the guy from the surveillance photos of the Ferrare compound. Although it was hard to tell much from snapshots, he'd guess the guy was a low-level thug in the security net around Ferrare. Probably had been sent out to chase away the man who'd shown up in Shannon's apartment unexpectedly.

He checked his clothes for blood. Fortunately his dark blue shirt didn't show the splatters from the other man much at all. He spat on his hands and picked up a handful of dirt, using it to scrub the worst of the blood from his hands.

"C'mon," he muttered. "Let's get out of here."

"Who are you?" she repeated more forcefully.

He sighed. "We've been over that already. Nothing's changed just because you've seen me do my job now. That guy could come back with help. We've got to go. Now." He put enough force behind his words to light a fire under her.

She lurched into motion, heading for the brighter street ahead.

When they turned back onto the main road, he fell in beside her. He asked gently, "Do you want to keep shopping, or would you rather head home?"

"You're kidding, right?" she snorted.

He shrugged. "We don't have a tail anymore. I took care of him back there." He jerked his chin toward the alley. "I doubt they've got a second man in the area to take over surveillance on us. And even if they do, as long as we stay out in a crowded place, their men won't mess with me. Too much possibility of collateral damage that could draw the police." His mouth turned down a little. "Plus, they don't know precisely how badass I am. They won't want to find that out with a bunch of witnesses around in case I kick their butts. It could wreck their street cred."

"What's that?"

"Their credibility on the street."

"Ahh. Their macho reputations."

"Exactly."

They walked awhile in silence. Then she asked, "What's

to keep them from breaking into my apartment tonight and killing us both?"

He replied calmly, "They won't know if I've booby-trapped the place or if I'm armed. They'll figure I'm some sort of professional. They just won't know what kind of professional I am. And until they do, they'll move with caution."

"And when they do? What then?"

"They're gonna have to search long and hard to learn anything about me. I all but don't exist outside of a few government databases, and even those are restricted access and say nothing about what I do. Long before then, I should be done with this gig."

On high alert, he gazed around the market, looking for the telltale movements of tails. Nada. He'd bet a year's salary, though, that the next time he and Shannon went out there'd be an entire team of Ferrare's top men trailing them.

That kid he'd roughed up would deliver his whispered message to Ferrare that a boy should not try to do a man's work. Although Shannon would never believe him, he'd actually taken it easy on the kid. He'd hit him in ways designed to cause maximum blood and swelling, but without doing any real damage. He hadn't broken any bones, no dislocated jaws or ribs, no concussions. The kid would hurt like hell for a few days, but he'd make a full recovery. Would probably think twice before he pulled a knife on someone again, too.

Shannon was unnaturally quiet beside him as they continued home. He had some serious damage control to do with her. But first things first. He pulled out his cell phone and called H.O.T. Watch Ops. Brady Hathaway answered the phone.

Jake said, "Hey. It's Howdy. Looks like things are heating up down here. Just had a little run-in with one of my target's low-level guys. Any chance I can get some backup in the near future?"

"Are you good for another twenty-four hours so I can gin

up a full team, or do I need to scramble a few men sooner than that?"

"I'm good for another day or two. If that changes, I'll give you a holler."

"Don't underestimate Ferrare, Howdy. He's smart and resourceful. Not too many people pull off rising from the dead."

"Speaking of that, any ideas how he did it?"

"Still working on it. We found the jeweler who made Ferrare's ring. Turns out he made a pair of matching rings. Jennifer's got a guy interviewing someone from Ferrare's dentist office as we speak. Whaddaya want to bet that two sets of dental records were kept in Ferrare's name? One for him and one for a double."

Howdy snorted. "I wouldn't take that bet for a plug nickel."

"How did the double end up fighting with Joe and dying in Joe's arms, then?"

Hathaway replied, "Joe says it was dark when Ferrare attacked him the night Ferrare's house blew up. He never got a real good look at the guy."

Memory of that fight flared clearly in Jake's head. He'd been watching the fight through the scope of his sniper rifle, silently begging Joe to give him a clear shot at Ferrare, in fact. Now that he thought about it, he'd never really gotten a good look at the man fighting Joe, either. He'd seen the ring, and the clothes, the general build and coloring and just assumed it was Ferrare. And then, without warning, the whole house blew up around the two men. Lit up like a torch. Wrecked his night vision and damn near blinded him for ten minutes.

Hathaway continued. "Joe said the explosion blew him and Ferrare—or Ferrare's double—apart. Joe landed in the swimming pool. Hit his head. Was knocked unconscious.

Floated on his back on top of some debris for several minutes."

Jake remembered that, too. Devastated, he'd run up to the house, sure that Joe was dead. And there he'd been, soaking wet, standing beside the swimming pool, hanging on to Ferrare's daughter like he was never going to let her go.

"The explosion blew Joe out the door, but the dynamic overpressure from the blast sucked Ferrare back into the house."

Jake nodded. Everyone had commented at the time how lucky Joe had been to land in the pool, where the inward collapse of air back into the vacuum created by the explosion couldn't suck him into the house fire.

"So you think Ferrare's double attacked Joe and died in the blast, but Ferrare made it out before the house blew up?"

"Have you got a better explanation?"

"Nope. It makes sense. Then Ferrare lays low for a while, lets people forget about him, and then goes back into business again very quietly. I gotta say, I'm glad to know there's a logical explanation of how the guy could still be alive."

Hathaway laughed at the other end of the line. "I'll let you know what the dentist says. But the body-double theory is looking good. Update me as you make progress and I'll get on that support team."

"Thanks."

He and Shannon were approaching her apartment building. He was tempted to duck around to the back entrance on the other side of the high-rise rather than stroll down the street in front of Ferrare's place as proud as you please. Thing was, he was supposed to have no idea that their would-be mugger worked for Ferrare, or that Ferrare was holed up behind that wall looming ahead.

His back muscles twitching violently, he guided Shannon down the street.

"Smile at me," he murmured.

"Why?"

"Just do it. Please?"

She did, although it looked patently fake. He sighed. "Did you hear the one about the chicken crossing the road?"

She blinked at him, surprised. "What are you doing?"

"Trying to make you laugh—or at least not look like you're about to puke."

"Is it that obvious?"

"Oh, yeah."

The rigidity went out of her spine. "I'm sorry."

It was the first sign of recovery from her after witnessing him beating up Ferrare's man. Hallelujah. Without once glancing at the walled fortress across the street, he ushered her into her building and the elevator. She sagged against the conveyance's back wall as it whooshed upward.

"You're doing great," he murmured. "Just a little bit farther. Don't fall apart on me until we get inside your place. Okay?"

The elevator dinged, and she took a deep breath. Stood up straight. Put on her game face. *Strong woman.* He truly wished her life had been such that she'd never had to learn how to be that way. But people didn't always get to pick the hand they were dealt. He didn't pick his father or the childhood he'd had. He'd just made the best of what skills he'd been given. And at least he wasn't a psychopath or serial killer. That was good for a tick or two in the reasons-not-to-send-him-to-hell column, wasn't it?

Shannon fumbled, her hands shaking too badly to get the key in the proper slot. Putting his hand smoothly over hers, he took the keys and eased them into the lock. He opened the door, let her pass and didn't bother to check for surveillance. He already knew it was there. He'd be shocked if Ferrare's informant on this floor hadn't already been called and told to keep an eagle eye on him.

Shannon made a beeline for her bedroom and closed the door behind her. He didn't try to follow. A hundred to one she'd gone into her bathroom and turned on the water to hide the sound of her having a good cry. Not that she didn't deserve it. It must've completely freaked her out to see him take down a guy like that. He didn't even want to contemplate the memories it must've conjured for her.

He'd give anything not to dredge up memories of her violent past, but what choice did he have? He cursed long and fluently under his breath. Sometimes this job purely sucked.

He made his way into the kitchen and stripped off his shirt, then washed as much of the blood off himself and out of the garment as he could. He hung it up to dry, then put away the groceries they'd purchased.

When she hadn't emerged from the bedroom an hour later he started cooking dinner. He whipped up a stew of fresh, local vegetables, chicken and savory spices. And suddenly he was the cat's best friend. He fed Mignette—it never hurt to be on friendly terms with the indigenous wildlife—put on a pot of rice to steam and chopped fruit into the biggest salad bowl he could find. He even dug out a tablecloth and candles.

It was pretty lame as apologies went, but he couldn't take her out to a bar and get her drunk on his tab like he would to apologize to one of his teammates. Women. Did they have to be so completely different from men?

Shannon blew her nose one last time and splashed cold water on her face to help bring down the puffiness around her eyes. She repaired her makeup and took a deep breath. She had to face Jake sooner or later. She just wished it could be much later.

Okay, so she'd known he was an operative of some kind

and his job included killing people. It shouldn't have surprised
her that he knocked that mugger into last week. In fact, she
hadn't even really been afraid when the guy jumped them
because she was so certain of Jake's skills. Why then, had she
completely flipped out when he used those skills to protect
her?

Easy. The look on his face. Or, rather, the lack of a look on
his face. He'd been completely composed. Calm. Unemotional.
Unaffected by beating the tar out of another human being. It
had been…inhuman.

Although on reflection, that probably shouldn't be a
surprise, either. It was his job. He did that kind of thing every
day. Or, if not every day, often enough that it obviously wasn't
a big deal to him. But he was one of the good guys, right?
That made it okay, right?

Then why did her gut clench in terror at the idea of leaving
the bathroom and going out to join him?

He was not Lucifer Jones. Not even close. Not even in the
same universe. Jake Harrington was a decent guy who did a
violent job. He was not a criminal. He only killed on orders
from above. But apparently, he could beat the crap out of
someone without permission.

She shuddered at the memory of blood flying every which
way and that poor man's whimpers. Tears welled up in her
eyes again. *Get a grip!* She could do this. She'd faced Lucifer
Jones in court. She'd learned how to live alone again. She slept
through the night most nights, now.

Resolutely, she marched out of the bathroom. Through
her bedroom. To the door. She hesitated with her hand on the
knob, but then she yanked the door open. Too late to chicken
out now. She stepped out into her living room.

And looked around in surprise. The lights were dim and
candles flickered on the dining table, which had been pulled
out into the middle of the space. Peruvian wood-pipe music

played softly in the background. Delicious smells were coming from her kitchen. And Jake was standing in front of her stove, stirring a pot of something savory and steaming. Shirtless and wearing an apron.

The guy couldn't look more domestic-sexy if he'd tried. He glanced up and about knocked her over by actually smiling at her.

"Get some rest?" he asked casually.

What on earth had she been so afraid of? This guy was no psychopathic killer. He was just a guy. Who did a nasty job by day and cooked dinner by night.

"Uhh, yes, I did. Thanks. I'm feeling better."

"Good. Dinner's ready. I hope you like paella."

"Sounds incredible. Particularly since I didn't have to make it."

"The sweet potatoes should be out of the oven in a few minutes, but I'll serve up the stew now if you're hungry."

She moved over to the table and sat down. Was she really this big a sucker? The guy made dinner and talked nice and she just melted? Or was it more a case of her simply having overreacted earlier? She supposed it was a distinct possibility.

He slipped into the bedroom and, to her disappointment, emerged wearing a clean shirt. He served up the meal, poured wine for each of them, then slid into the chair across from her. "Bon appétit," he murmured.

She nodded and dug in. The guy could seriously cook. "This is wonderful."

"Thanks. It's a favorite of mine. By the way, don't get the wrong impression. I only know how to cook about three things."

She laughed and sipped her wine. "Duly noted. What are the other two?"

"They involve wild animals not readily available in this part of the world."

She made a face. "I'll pass on those."

He grinned. "It's amazing how many things are edible that most Americans wouldn't dream of trying. But when a person's hungry enough, just about anything can become a meal."

That sounded like the voice of experience speaking. She asked quietly, "How often were you that hungry as a kid?"

He shrugged. "Depended on how the hunting was going. My dad and I were both pretty good at it, but now and then we hit dry spells. Hunger focuses a person on a task like hunting like just about nothing else in this world."

"I bet."

He laid down his spoon. "About this afternoon, Shannon…"

She glanced up at him apprehensively.

"I'm sorry you had to see that."

"Me, too." She took a deep breath and asked the question that had been niggling at her ever since they'd gotten home. "Tell me something. Was it necessary to…subdue him…quite that violently?"

Jake leaned back and took a long sip of the wine. "I suppose it wouldn't help my case if I told you I took it easy on him, would it?"

"You call that easy?" she exclaimed.

He sighed. "That's what I thought you'd say. Yeah. That was easy. I made sure he looked bad because I wanted to send a message to Ferrare not to mess with us. But I didn't really hurt the guy. Lots of soft tissue damage and blood, but no broken bones or concussions."

She gave him her best skeptical look.

"What would you have had me do, Shannon? Let him assault us? Rob us? Slice us up?"

She frowned.

He leaned forward, pressing the point. "How much harm should I have allowed him to do first before I fought back?"

When he put it that way, she found it hard to argue against him. "It was just so bloody."

"Street fights usually are. They can turn deadly fast. Had he been any good with that knife, I'd likely have been nearly as bloody as him."

She glanced up, and in the shadowed candlelight had no trouble envisioning him with his face covered in bloody gashes. The image made her nauseous.

"Shannon. Do you seriously think I could have stood by and let him hurt you?"

Touché. She sighed. "All right. I get it. You did what you had to, and I overreacted."

He smiled and refilled her glass, gracious in victory. "I don't blame you for reacting like you did. I'm sorry if I brought back any unpleasant memories for you."

She lifted the glass and took a long drink.

"Am I forgiven?"

She studied him over the rim of her glass. Forgiven. An interesting concept in relation to him. A man who killed people without the slightest shred of remorse. She'd bet forgiveness was something he didn't get from people very often. What about from himself? Did he forgive himself for what he did?

She shrugged. "Sure. You're forgiven. But at the end of the day, it doesn't really matter what I think of today's events, now does it? What really matters is what you think of it all."

"Come again?"

"What do you think about having beat that guy to a pulp?"

He frowned. "I assume you're not talking about the tactical implications of one of Ferrare's low-level thugs testing us?"

"No. I'm talking about how you feel. Not what you think. How do you *feel* about it?"

Chapter 9

Jake resorted to getting up and carrying a batch of dishes into the kitchen to avoid answering her question. How did he feel? He never thought about such things. Feelings were *not* healthy in his line of work. But damned if this woman didn't arouse all kinds of feelings in him.

She'd looked so beautiful sitting across the table from him with the candlelight caressing her face. Like some sort of goddess of femininity. And she was a complete mystery to him, with all her tears and fears and *feelings*.

He washed dishes with a vengeance until it occurred to him that he was succumbing to anger. He finished up, swearing under his breath. Shannon was sitting on the sofa reading a book when he emerged from the kitchen.

"I'm going to rest a little bit before tonight," he announced.

She glanced up from her book. "Okay."

Inexplicably irritated at her lack of interest, he folded

his legs and sat down on the thick area rug in front of her television. Crossing his legs Indian-style, he closed his eyes and commenced counting backward from one hundred.

"What are you doing?" Her voice tore him from his quiet.

He opened one eye. "Meditating."

"*You* meditate?"

"When I'm not being interrupted, I do."

"Sorry." He thought he heard her mutter under her breath, "Sourpuss."

He sighed. Opened his eyes. "I'm sorry I snapped at you."

She nodded her forgiveness and subsided. Closing his eyes again, he picked up counting where he'd left off. Calm flowed over him and through him.

"Are you always this tense on missions?" Her question yanked him out of the calm once again.

"I'm not tense," he replied.

"Huh. I'd hate to see you when you think you're wired."

"If you'll let me do this meditation, I promise I'll emerge from it the soul of calm."

"This I have to see. Proceed."

He responded dryly, "Thanks. I will."

He closed his eyes a third time. This time he made it all the way through his countdown and relaxation sequence. But at the end of it, he was so vividly aware, even through his closed eyelids, of her gaze riveted upon him that he couldn't shut off the noise in his mind. The woman was a menace. Not only did she bombard him with her feelings, but she projected her disquiet onto him as well.

He sat there for several more minutes, berating himself for letting her get to him like this. He was an island. A rock…

…not a rock. A sponge, dammit.

It was no use. The woman had him so discombobulated

he couldn't even begin to achieve his shooter's calm. *Women. Menaces, one and all.* He sighed and opened his eyes.

"Feeling better?" she asked archly.

He lied. "Yes, thank you." After all, he'd promised her calm. If he couldn't feel it, he could at least fake it.

"Maybe you'd like a shower? You didn't get a chance to this afternoon, since I had the bathroom, uhh, tied up."

He glanced over at his cameras, sitting on the windowsill now nested under a half-dozen cactus plants. "I washed up in the kitchen earlier. And I can't leave the cameras unattended."

"I'll watch them for you."

He looked over at her in surprise. "You'd do that for me?"

"Sure. Why not? If you're living in my house, I may as well be of some use. What do I do?"

He motioned her over to his laptop. They crowded in front of it, and he did his damnedest to ignore how good she smelled. All fresh and shampooed and perfumed.

He explained, "If any of the alarms go off, highlight the window on my laptop like this, then click this button here to record the images."

"That's it?"

He shrugged. "The hard part is the computer programming to make it easy for field schmucks like me to use."

She guffawed. "You're as smart as they come, and don't even try to fool me into thinking otherwise, buster."

Grinning, he retreated to the bathroom. His shower was quick but incredibly refreshing. Bathing in the middle of a surveillance op was a luxury he'd never experienced before. And he had to say it was pretty nice. Feeling a hundred percent better, he emerged into the living room.

"Any alarms from the cameras while I was gone?"

"Not a peep."

She stood up from in front of his computer, and he moved to take her place. They passed chest to chest, and she glanced up at him wide-eyed in awareness. Girl-noticing-boy awareness. Holy…

His brain locked up. He couldn't very well blurt out what was actually going through his mind, for it involved dragging her back to the bedroom and exploring the scents of her much more thoroughly.

"Thanks for the shower," he mumbled. "It was great."

"You're welcome," she replied, all breathy and sexy. Good Lord. She sounded like she was thinking about exactly the same thing he was! His hands started to rise to touch her face. To tuck that strand of dark hair behind her ear. Hell, to rip her clothes off and pull her beneath him.

Apparently, she must be psychic because her face lit up in a fiery blush. "Uhh, I think I'm going to call it a night. It has been a big day."

Jake nodded. Images of her naked and sprawled in her bed were so powerful in his mind he couldn't form casual words of response. She disappeared into the bedroom but didn't close the door behind her. He all but groaned aloud. If she knew what was good for her, she'd lock that thing and barricade it with her dresser.

Shannon emerged again carrying an armload of bedding. "Here's a blanket, pillow and sheets. If the couch isn't long enough for you, maybe you can make yourself a bed on the rug."

He blinked. A shower and clean sheets in the middle of an op? He took the bedding from her in minor shock.

The next few hours passed in a haze for him. He made up a bed on the sofa, set his cameras to give him an audible warning anytime they sensed movement and then he stretched out. This was bar none the most comfortable hide he'd even been on. By a mile. By a thousand miles.

However, sleep was *not* happening. Every time he closed his eyes, Shannon's face came to him, her voice murmuring, *How do you feel, Jake?* Swear to God, it gave him cold sweats just to contemplate it.

Finally, he got up and resumed his position behind the draperies, gazing out at the Ferrare compound below. The main yard was quiet, but lights blazed through the windows like the household hadn't retired for the night yet. Five years ago, Ferrare hadn't been a particular night owl. Unless he had a late business meeting, of course. Middle of the night, clandestine late. Hmm.

He moved over to the table and his laptop to review all the tapes the computer had captured during the day. He compiled images of everyone who'd come and gone from the compound and forwarded those to Carter Baigneaux to identify. But in the context of the tapes, it all looked like the usual comings and goings of a house with a dozen or more people living in it.

He sat back down in the middle of the living room and went through his meditation regimen again. Without Shannon there to provide running commentary, he was somewhat more successful this time at achieving a state of calm. It wasn't his usual icy chill, but it was better than nothing.

He'd been back at the window making like a statue for a couple of hours when a cry from the other room startled him into violent motion. He raced into the bedroom, ready to kill whoever or whatever was attacking Shannon.

Shannon thrashed beneath the covers. Quick scan. No intruders. He quickly checked under the bed and in the bathroom and walk-in closet. No one. Daring to breathe, he cleared the room a second time, more thoroughly and slowly. She was alone in here. Crisis past, his heart erupted into a staccato of uneven thumps.

Christ, that woman did things to him no one else had ever come close to.

She cried out again. Thrashed some more. She was having a nightmare. Should he wake her up from it or just let her sleep it off? If he was lucky, she wouldn't remember anything in the morning.

"Please, Mr. Jones. No! I'll do anything you say...." Terror vibrated thickly in her voice. Sick knowledge of the torture to come. "Do what you want. Just don't kill—"

That was all he could take. Jake touched Shannon's shoulder. "Wake up, honey. You're having a nightmare."

She lurched to a sitting position, and he yanked his hand back. She looked around wildly. "Huh? Where...wha..."

"You were having a bad dream. Just a dream," he soothed.

"Lucifer." She flopped back down to the bed, breathing heavily. "I haven't dreamed about him in a long time. Must've been the attack today that triggered it. That, and the fact that he's out of jail."

It felt like she'd reached into his belly and ripped his guts out. *He* was responsible for that raw, tearing fear in her voice. He muttered, "I'm so sorry. It's all my fault."

She reached up and touched his cheek. He froze, stunned at the contact. "It's not your fault. You didn't climb in my window and terrorize me."

"No. I just knocked on your front door and strolled right in."

"You're nothing like him, Jake. Trust me."

"You sure about that?" he asked roughly. She hadn't been so sure of it earlier today.

He thought she smiled faintly in the dark. "That dream reminded me what he was like. You might have felt nothing when you were beating up that guy, but Lucifer enjoyed doing it to me."

Rage consumed Jake so fast he didn't stand a chance of halting it. His fists clenched until they shook, and he had to take several deep breaths to keep from hitting the wall. He'd kill the guy. That was all there was to it.

Shannon reared back in alarm, and that was probably the only thing that checked him from heading out her front door and commencing hunting down one Lucifer Jones with the intent to murder him in cold blood.

Right now she didn't need his anger. She needed his calm. His reassurance. He released the rage, letting it flow through him and out of him like a flood draining from behind a dam.

"Are you going to be able to go back to sleep?" he asked gently.

"I don't know. Is this the part where you crawl in beside me and comfort me and we take our relationship to the next level?"

Whoa. Brain freeze.

He didn't know where to begin to react to that one. Relationship? Them? Crawl in with her? Comfort her? Next level? *What the hell was the next level?*

He answered more sharply than he'd intended. "No. This is the part where I go back to my post and resume watching the bad guy, and you go back to sleep."

"Oh."

Cripes. Did she have to sound so disappointed? He felt like he'd just kicked a puppy. Aww, hell. He was about an inch from doing exactly as she'd suggested, and there was no doubt whatsoever that would be an unmitigated disaster.

It was an act of extreme discipline to force himself to smile at her. Turn away. Put one foot in front of the other until he'd gained the safety of her living room. To head over to the corner. Tuck himself in behind the drapes. Stare blindly out the window at he knew not what.

He had no idea how long he stood there. It wasn't long enough to erase the images from his mind of "next levels." With Shannon. In her bed. Now. Waiting and willing for him to join her. Hell, he'd probably just set back her recovery from her ordeal by a year by turning down her invitation to cuddle... and whatever else she'd had in mind.

Frustrated, he stretched out on the sofa and tossed and turned, the sheets hot and rumpled.

The bedroom door burst open without warning.

He sat up fast, hand on his weapon. "What's wrong?" he asked quickly, searching over her shoulder for threats.

She marched over to him like a little girl playing soldier. "This is what's wrong."

She reached down, grabbed him by both shoulders and kissed him. Not a how-do-you-do kiss. A wet, open-mouthed, tongue-down-his-throat, I-want-to-do-naughty-things-to-you-right-now sort of kiss.

What the—

"Shannon!" he mumbled against her mouth.

"Shut up and kiss me."

All right, then. His arms swept up around her, pulling her down on top of him. Her body was so soft and warm and sexy he skipped a breath. She had curves in all the right places, and they felt out of this world smashed against him.

Her hands came up and slid around his neck, her fingers tangling in his hair and pulling him closer and deeper into their kiss. Her thigh rode up between his, rubbing parts of him that were more than willing to leap to attention and did so with alacrity. Her whole body writhed, undulating against him as she slanted her mouth across his, devouring him like she couldn't get enough of him.

She came up for air at some point, and he fell back gasping, but then she came after him again, and he was completely helpless to resist her. She was no kitten. She was a lioness.

On the hunt. And he was her meal of choice. But what a way to go. He sank into the kiss, surrendering himself to it with abandon. His hands roamed up and down her back, learning the contours of her, the sensitive places, the firm and soft places of her body.

Her hands crept up under his shirt, warm against his bare skin. He'd love to reciprocate, but some vestige of caution, of need not to frighten her, held him back. She kissed her way across his chest until he groaned, then nibbled her way up his neck and back to his mouth.

And finally, about a year later, she raised her head to look down at him. "There. Now you don't have to lie awake all night fearing that."

She shoved up and away from him, and he stared at her incredulously. "Why on earth would I fear that?"

"I dunno. You might actually have to *feel* something," she retorted with light sarcasm.

He laughed. "Honey, I'm happy to feel that way every day and twice on Sunday."

She planted her hands on her hips. "Then the next time I invite you to snuggle with me and comfort me after a bad dream, don't run away from me."

"Yes, ma'am."

"I'm serious."

"So am I."

She turned to head for the bedroom. She took about three steps and then stopped to look over her shoulder. "Are you coming with me or not?"

Was she... Did she... His brain had to quit freezing up like this. She was going to think he was mentally impaired. And he wasn't dumb enough to make the lady ask again. He leaped to his feet.

She smiled and disappeared into the bedroom and he was right on her heels. He made it as far as the doorway before a warning tone sounded from his laptop. He paused, frowning, not immediately computing what that annoying sound meant.

Then it hit him. He swore under his breath.

Someone was moving over at the Ferrare estate. And it was the middle of the freaking night. This could not be normal activity. He swore aloud as he veered away from the bedroom. *Damn, damn, damn. This had better be good.*

What the hell was Ferrare up to now?

Chapter 10

Swearing under his breath, Jake moved over to his computer. A big, swanky vehicle had just pulled through the front gate of the Ferrare compound and set off one of his motion detectors. Another alarm sounded. His camera pointed at the front door had sensed it opening. Two burly men stepped out, and Jake's pulse quickened. He recognized both men—bodyguard types from the look of them—from the photographs of Eduardo Ferrare several weeks ago.

A third man stepped outside.

Bingo.

Jake stared in disbelief at the man strolling toward the now-stopped limousine. Intellectually, he knew Ferrare was alive. But his gut still rebelled at the freakish sight of a man whom he'd watched die walking around casually talking and gesturing to his men. The guy moved just like the Eduardo Ferrare of old. The same arrogance. The same command of everyone and everything around him. The same alert attention to every detail within eyesight. *This was not the double. This was the real Eduardo Ferrare.*

And his sniper gun was sitting in his duffel bag, useless. He'd been so involved with Shannon that Ferrare had caught him completely unprepared. Cursing himself thoroughly, Jake weighed sprinting for his shooting rig or staying put and watching the unfolding action below.

The limousine door opened. Two big men armed to the teeth stepped out. They spoke briefly with Ferrare's henchmen and then took up positions at the front and rear fenders of the vehicle, automatic weapons at the ready, their gazes roaming constantly.

Four more men, obviously the principals, stepped out of the long, sleek vehicle. Jake quickly captured stills of them on his computer and fired them off electronically to H.O.T. Watch headquarters with an identity query. Personally, he didn't recognize any of them. They carried themselves like wealthy, powerful men. Their custom-tailored, perfectly pressed suits gave away the wealth part, and the way the guards tensed in their presence gave away the power part. What was Ferrare up to?

A new alarm sounded on Jake's computer. The front-gate motion detector again. Another limousine was just rounding the corner into the compound. The first limo's guards didn't react, so obviously this second vehicle was expected. Jake watched with interest to see who emerged from this car. Maybe the next few minutes would answer the question of what Ferrare was planning.

The second set of men was much like the first, although the men were slightly younger, wore shorter hair and generally moved more athletically. He frowned. In fact, the second set of men moved like military types. What would Gavronese Army men want with Eduardo Ferrare? He was a drug dealer. The Gavronese government had always opposed him and his illegal empire vigorously. An icy chill crawled across the back of Jake's neck. This was not good. Not good at all. He didn't usually go much for instinct or intuition, but this time both were screaming at him in a way he couldn't ignore.

The group of men moved into the house. He sent a second batch of images to H.O.T. Watch, took a time hack on his watch and then hunkered down to the business of waiting. For the first time since he'd set foot in Shannon's apartment, the trancelike calm he usually brought to a mission flowed over him. Time ceased to have meaning. Mignette came and went, lying on his feet for a while, then growing tired of his poor company. Shannon conspicuously remained in her room. She must be pissed. He sighed. No help for it.

Sometime later his secure cell phone vibrated, and he flipped it on. "Howdy here," he muttered.

"This is Brady. We've been analyzing the pictures you sent us."

"And?"

"You know any of these guys?"

"I can tell you without a shadow of a doubt that the man in that compound is the original Eduardo Ferrare. It must have been his double that died five years ago."

"How certain are you of that?" he asked sharply.

"I'd bet my life on it. And if he showed himself tonight like this, he's very, very close to his end goal."

A long silence greeted that. Finally, he asked, "Recognize any of his visitors?"

"Nope. But that second batch of guests was military."

"Why do you say that?" Hathaway sounded surprised.

"The way they moved. The way the guards deferred to them. The way they stood erect and didn't slouch. Have your analysts play back the video of them and they'll see what I mean. These guys are not only military, but they're officers. High-ranking if I don't miss my guess."

"We don't have a video feed right now. The only satellite we've got available tonight feeds us still frames every fifteen seconds or so."

"That's why you've got me here on the ground, Brady. I can see what a satellite can't. And I'm telling you, these guys carry themselves and move like military. I'll send you some video footage from my surveillance cameras. You'll see."

He laughed. "All right, already. I believe you. I'll relay your video and your opinions to Carter. He's already running faces through his magic face-recognition software. Any people he can't identify I'll run past an expert we brought in earlier this evening to help make identifications of Gavronese nationals."

"Lemme know what you come up with," Jake replied.

"Will do. Stay out of sight of these guys, eh?"

He disconnected without bothering to reply. He knew the rules of engagement. Hell, he'd written some of them. A soft sound of distress startled him. *Shannon.* He leaped to his feet and raced into her bedroom, every killing sense on full alert.

"Jake…Jake…" she mumbled.

"I'm here," he whispered.

She didn't answer. He peered at her in the dark. She was asleep. Dammit. At least she was dreaming about him. He supposed that was good news at any rate—stop. Back up. Cease that line of reasoning. It didn't matter one damned bit if she was dreaming about him. They were *not* a they. Not an item. Not a couple. They were exactly nothing. End of discussion.

Not the end! a little voice in the back of his head argued. *"They" are just beginning!*

Shut up, Self.

Great. Now he was listening to the voices in his head. And worse, he was talking back to them.

She looked like a little girl with her fist tucked under her chin and hair spilling across her face. An innocent to whom nothing bad should ever happen. An urge to wrap her up in a protective cocoon and never let her out came over him. If she were his woman, nothing bad would ever happen to her again.

He had to forget about her. Get his head back in the game. He was here to nail Ferrare.

You want her. Admit it. And why not make her your woman? You know you could do it if you put your mind to it.

Shut. Up. Self.

But no matter how sternly he lectured it, that damned voice in the back of his head flatly refused to listen. This was definitely on the list of symptoms he was supposed to report to his superiors immediately after he removed himself from the field and handed over all of his weapons. Oh, well. So much for proper military procedure. Good thing he'd never gotten too wrapped around the axle about such things. He was tight enough when it came to the business of killing, but the other military stuff? The spit shines and gig lines and high-and-tight hair? They were good for instilling basic discipline in eighteen-year-old kids. But they didn't do a hell of lot for him at this point in his career. His personal discipline came from deep inside him, so deep he couldn't even put his finger on its source.

Shannon mumbled again.

Should he wake her up? Pick up where they'd left off when she'd laid that incendiary kiss on him? As tempting at that was, he elected to let her sleep. She'd had a rough day. Emotionally draining. She'd earned a decent night's rest. Although the way she was tossing and turning, he wasn't sure how restful it really was. He sighed. Lifted the sheet carefully. Slid in beside her. She was probably going to wake up, whip out his pistol from under her pillow and shoot him dead. And he'd probably deserve it.

He'd stay for just a minute. Just until she settled down. After all, he needed to get back out into the living room and his cameras.

He reached out and touched her bare shoulder with a single finger. No reaction. He laid his entire palm lightly against her skin. It slid under his fingertips like the finest velvet. He couldn't remember ever feeling anything quite so smooth and soft. It was as if her very essence seeped into him. He couldn't resist leaning down to touch his lips to a spot just over her right shoulder blade. She murmured vaguely, but settled quickly.

He let his hand slide slowly down her arm. Goosebumps popped up on his arms at the sensation. But she stayed safely asleep. His hand cupped her elbow then followed the slender line of her forearm until his arm wrapped loosely about her. Calling on every ounce of his extraordinary discipline, he eased forward by millimeters until his chest barely touched her back. Still no reaction from her. He moved a tiny bit more. His entire front was now spooned around her warm, sweet-scented body. He'd have groaned in pleasure if he didn't think the sound would've woken her.

And then a miracle happened. She leaned back slightly, snuggling against him. Her hand came over his at her waist, pulling his arm more securely around her as if he were a blanket wrapping her in warmth. Wonder exploded in his brain. Somewhere in her unconscious mind, she trusted him. After everything she'd been through in her life, after he'd scared the living daylights out of her by attacking her, after she'd witnessed the worst sort of violence out of him...some part of her trusted him.

He didn't deserve it.

His entire being recoiled from the feel of her body, the scent of her femininity, the drugging pull of her. He didn't deserve her softness, her kindness, not her skin against his, not her hand resting lightly on his, none of it. He was a killer, not a human being. A *monster*.

Revulsion at everything he was, everything he'd ever done, washed over him. He was filthy. Unworthy of touching Shannon, let alone holding her in his arms. He let go of her, easing away from her, leaving her to her innocent dreams.

She groaned. Shifted in her sleep. Then mumbled, "Don't go."

He froze. She was asleep. Didn't know what she was saying. And even if she did know, he still didn't deserve to be in the same universe with her. He resumed moving, easing out of the bed until he stood beside her. She was still once more.

Words drifted through his mind. He was too distraught to know whether he whispered them aloud or not. "Sweet dreams, Shannon. I wish like hell I was a good enough man for you. But I'm not."

He turned silently and strode from the room.

Shannon opened her eyes and watched him go. The ache in his whispered words broke her heart. Why on earth didn't he think he was good enough for her? He was an amazing man. He did a job that would have destroyed her, and he was still whole. Well, maybe not whole. But not entirely broken, either.

She closed her eyes. Tried to go back to sleep. But Jake's whispered words kept rolling through her mind, haunted and desolate. She couldn't do it. She couldn't ignore his pain. She threw back the sheets, yanked the thin strap of her nightgown back up onto her shoulder and marched out into the living room.

Jake looked up in surprise and chagrin. "I'm sorry. I woke you up, didn't I?"

"Yes, you did. Why didn't you stay like I asked?" she replied.

He stared at her in what could only be open shock. "I beg your pardon?" he finally mumbled.

"You heard me. Why didn't you stay?"

"Shannon, I'm here to do a job. Not seduce the nice lady who let me use her apartment for a few days."

"Don't give me that crap, Jake Harrington. If you're going to avoid me, at least tell me the truth about why."

That made him stare. And she supposed it should. Where this sudden boldness had come from in her, she had no idea. Or maybe she did have an idea. It came from feeling safe. When she was with this man, certainty came over her that nothing bad would ever touch her. It was ridiculous, but true nonetheless.

He leaned back in his chair and studied her for long enough that she felt an urge to squirm. "Why don't you tell me why I'm avoiding you if you know so much about me?"

She walked over to stand in front of him, vividly aware of how thin and fragile her cotton nightgown was. It floated over her body like mist dissipating fast under the heat of his stare.

"I think you're scared of me," she announced.

He snorted.

She pressed the point. "I think you're scared of women. Of feeling good. Heck, I think you're scared to be happy."

"Honey, I'll admit there are a few things in this world that do scare me, but you are not one of them."

She took a step closer. It registered in the back of her mind that she was now in range of his powerful hands, of that lethal quickness that had struck with cobralike accuracy today at that guy in the alley. "You are such a bad liar."

His silver gaze narrowed, glittering with irritation.

She glared back. "You've got this stupid notion that you don't deserve to be happy, and that's a load of hooey."

"Hooey?" he echoed in amusement. "Is that some regional phrase common to Gavarone that I've never heard of?"

"Don't try to change the subject on me. You know I'm right."

Abruptly, all humor evaporated from him, leaving him as grim and fierce as she'd ever seen him. "Fine. You're right. In my line of work, happiness is not part of the deal. And I'm okay with that."

"Well, I'm not okay with it," she retorted.

One brown eyebrow cocked over that icy cold stare of his. "Not my problem," he bit out.

She reached out with her right index finger and poked him in the shoulder. "Cut the crap, Jake. You've got this notion that you don't deserve to have the happiness the rest of us human beings spend our lives pursuing. And it's a stupid notion."

His voice went flat. Deadly calm. "Are you calling me stupid?"

A flutter of trepidation warned her that she might be pushing this man too far. But something reckless inside her had broken loose since he crawled into bed with her and held her so gently, and no amount of common sense was enough to hold it back. "I'm calling you worse than stupid. You're an intelligent man who's willfully choosing to act stupid."

He surged to his feet, which placed him approximately two inches from her, and gritted from between clenched teeth, "You don't know anything about me."

Sadness washed over her. She gazed up at him compassionately. "I know you're not happy. I know you refuse to let yourself be happy. And I know you're dying inside. It may be happening slowly, bit by bit, but you're killing yourself, Jake."

His cold control broke then, and boiling fury rolled off of him. He didn't move, though. Not a single muscle twitched. They stood inches away from one another, and not one part

of him touched her. It might as well have been the Grand
Canyon yawning between them. How he got words past all
that rippling jaw muscle, she had no idea. But he ground out,
"I'm already dead."

And with that, he exploded into motion, whirling away
from her and striding over to the window to look down on
the Ferrare compound. Even so mad he could break her neck
with his bare hands, she noted that he glided like a ghost as
he approached the window, fading into the shadows as if he
were part of the night itself.

She'd lost him. Whatever chance she'd had to reach him
tonight, to break through those awful walls he'd built around
himself, was gone. Dejected, she turned and headed for her
lonely bed. She crawled under the covers and lay down, staring
up at the faint glow of a streetlight on her ceiling. She might
have lost this battle, but she wasn't giving up on the war. Not
by a long shot.

Chapter 11

Shannon didn't remember falling asleep, but she was ripped from slumber by a piercing screech that brought her bolt upright in bed. What on earth was that? Belatedly, her brain caught up with her reflexes. The building's fire alarm. Uh-oh. The St. George Fire Department wasn't exactly known for its spectacular capabilities.

She rushed into the living room, startled to see Jake affixing some sort of lock to the armoire in the corner. With a drill. And a hammer. "What are you doing?" she exclaimed. "You're ruining my cabinet!"

"I'll buy you a new one," he bit out. He picked up his duffel bags. "Let's go."

"I can't. Minnie."

"Who?" He gave her an uncomprehending look laced with exasperation.

"The cat."

He rolled his eyes. "It's probably not a real fire, anyway.

My money's on Ferrare's men to be emptying the building so they can search your apartment."

On her hands and knees, looking for the missing cat, Shannon glanced up at him. "Have you ever heard of a thing called paranoia?"

"It's not paranoia if bad men are really after you," he retorted.

"Help me find the cat," she ordered.

"Oh, for crying out loud." He rolled his eyes but did as she asked. She pushed to her feet and headed for Mignette's hiding place of last resort—the kitchen pantry. If the door wasn't securely latched, the feline could force her way in there. Sure enough, the door was open a few inches.

"Aha! There you are, bad kitty." She reached gently for the frightened cat. A paw swiped viciously at her, catching her across the back of the wrist. Were there not a fire alarm screaming overhead, she'd have retreated from Mignette. But as it was, she reached through the gauntlet of claws and grabbed the big cat.

"Have you got something to put that beast in?" Jake asked from the kitchen doorway.

"Hall closet. Floor. Cat carrier," she panted, wrestling with the furious animal.

"Coming up."

Jake was back in a second, which was a good thing, because Mignette was having no part of cooperating. Shannon stuffed the cat in the carrier, suffering a painful bite on her thumb for her troubles. Jake was already standing by the front door. He tested the knob with the back of his hand. It must not have been hot, for he opened the door a crack.

"No smoke," he announced. "Out you go."

"What? You're not coming?"

"Nope. I'm staying here to guard the surveillance equipment."

"But what if there's really a fire?" she cried.

"Then tell the fire department to send a ladder up to your living-room window."

"This isn't a joke, Jake—"

"Save it. I don't need you here when Ferrare's goons come calling."

She stared at him in dismay. He sounded serious. He *looked* serious.

"Go, Shannon. You'll only be in my way."

His voice crackled with sharp command, and his expression was implacable. She knew a losing battle when she saw one. She sighed, clutched Mignette's carrier more tightly, and stepped outside.

Jake's voice floated out beneath the screech of the fire alarm, which was even louder out here. "Don't use the elevator."

"I knew that," she muttered back as she moved off down the hall. Her neighbors were streaming toward the stairwell at the end, and she joined them, hating the panic vibrating in the air. The stairwell was even more crowded, and she shuffled down the metal steps, buffeted by the mob until she thought she might get knocked down.

She burst outside into the muggy night. A breeze was cool on her shoulders, and it dawned on her she was wearing only a flimsy cotton nightgown. Thankfully, many of her neighbors weren't wearing much more. She looked around for fire trucks and spotted none. Instead, she spotted something much scarier. Men. With guns. Big guns. Circling the crowd almost as if they were guarding it. Or searching it.

For her? For Jake? Either way, she didn't plan to make their job any easier. Her skin crawled as the men's hard gazes raked the crowd. She ducked behind a couple huddling together under a blanket, then slid deeper into the mass of milling humanity.

And maybe that was why she spotted the huge silhouette before he spotted her. Horror washed over her, hot and sickening. It couldn't be. Not Lucifer. She peeked around a woman from upstairs to where the giant form had been a moment ago. Gone.

Shannon straightened up, searching frantically. Where did he go? Not knowing was worse than having to look at him! She spun in a full circle, panic choking her. Still no sign of him. Had she imagined it? She felt naked. Alone. Where was Jake when she needed him, anyway? She'd give anything to be with him right now.

Lucifer. Here. For her. Her skin crawled.

Jake. She needed Jake. She looked frantically at the building. No smoke was coming from it. Only, a phalanx of armed men was keeping everyone from going back inside. The men were shouting for everyone to stay put until the fire department cleared the building. But the fire department wasn't on the scene. She didn't even hear sirens in the distance. Personally, she'd rather brave a raging fire than face Lucifer Jones.

Jake watched through the peephole as people walked and ran past Shannon's door for a minute or so after she left. He fought an urge to go after her and stick close by where he could keep an eye on her. It felt weird being separated from her like this. Which alarmed him mightily. He didn't get attached to anyone or anything. Never had.

The halls emptied. Now was when he would get company. He stepped away from the door in the dark, fading into the deepest shadows between the armoire and the curtains. He gripped the baseball bat he'd found in the back of Shannon's closet when he'd fished out the cat carrier and settled in to wait.

Sure enough, about thirty seconds later Shannon's door

knob rattled. He'd taken the chain off to make entry into her place easy. He was very interested to see who joined him tonight.

A lone figure slipped inside. Male. Dressed in black. Moving confidently. The guy headed straight for the living-room window. Definitely checking for surveillance equipment, then. He let the guy approach within about five feet, then leaped out swinging the bat. It connected with a solid thud, clocking the guy in the back of the head. Poor sucker never saw the blow coming. He just dropped like a stone at Jake's feet.

Jake hauled the inert form up and across his shoulders in a fireman's carry. Staggering a little under the guy's weight, Jake hustled to the door and out into the hall. He looked left and right and headed for the elevators. Thankfully, he only had to wait a few seconds for one to arrive. He punched the button for the sixth floor, one floor up from Shannon's place. The elevator door opened, and he stepped out, jogging heavily down the hall to the unit directly above Shannon's. He tested the door knob. Unlocked. Luck was with him tonight. He let himself in and carried the unconscious man over to the living-room window. After dumping the guy on the floor, he looked around hastily. This place had a shelf unit on the wall adjacent to the window. It was a little far away for his purposes, but it would have to do. He spotted a heavy vase sitting on the floor in the corner. He picked it up, carried it over to the crumpled man and smashed the pottery pot to the floor beside the guy. It shattered into dozens of pieces. He took a handful of the clay powder and shards littering the floor and rubbed them in the man's hair directly over the spot where he'd hit the guy with the bat.

There. Let people think the vase had fallen off the shelf, hit him in the head and knocked him out. Poor guy'd probably be too busy explaining to Ferrare why he'd gone into the right apartment on the wrong floor to worry too much about how he'd gotten knocked out.

Jake hurried back into the hall. He didn't put it past Ferrare to send more than one man in to investigate the American woman's place. He still couldn't hear sirens responding to the fire alarm, so the game wasn't over yet. This time he used the stairwell at the end of the hall, racing down its deserted turns to the fifth floor. Down the hall to Shannon's place and—

He froze. He hadn't left her door open. But it was definitely cracked a few inches wide now. He reached for his ankle holster and pulled out his spare service pistol. He nudged the door with his foot. No response. He opened the door fast, spinning in low and flattening himself against the wall just inside in a crouch. Movement. In the bedroom.

He raced across the living room and swept inside the bedroom, running in a zig-zag pattern toward the second intruder. He swung his pistol up into firing position and—

Crap. Shannon. He jerked the muzzle of his gun up and away from her at the last second before he blew her head off. "What are you doing here?" he growled.

"Jake!" she cried. She flew into his arms, heedless of the weapon in his right hand. Her arms wrapped around his neck, and in short order, she was half choking him to death.

"I've got you," he murmured, his arms coming up to pull her close. "Why did you come back?"

"He's out there. At least I think he's out there. I thought I saw him, but when I looked again, he was gone. But I could feel him close by and I had to get back to you. I knew you'd keep me safe. You'd know what to do…."

"What are you talking about, honey? Who did you see? Ferrare?"

"No. Lucifer."

A curse exploded from him. "Are you sure?"

"No. I'm not sure. And he disappeared. That's why I came back inside."

"Where's the cat?"

"Her carrier's in the living room."

"Let's get both of you out of here. The building could still burn down."

"I'm not going without you," she announced. "If you stay here, so do I."

He closed his eyes in chagrin. Stubborn determination had permeated her voice. He answered with thin patience, "I can't be responsible for you. For your safety."

She gave him an uncomprehending look. "But I trust you."

Under any other circumstances, he'd have done handsprings to hear those words from her. He spoke slowly and clearly. "I need you to go."

She spoke back just as slowly and clearly. "I'm not going without you."

He was wasting precious time here. "If I walk you out, have a look at the crowd for Lucifer and don't spot him, can I come back inside alone?"

She frowned, obviously not sold on that plan.

Dammit. "Fine. I'll go out with you. But we've got to hurry." He'd worry about ditching her outside and sneaking back inside to guard his equipment later. One problem at a time. "C'mon." He picked up the cat carrier, and a cloud of white hair flew out at him. He sneezed, and cat hair coated his front. Sheesh. The animal was a shedding machine.

He hustled Shannon down the hall and raced down the stairs with her close on his heels. He still didn't see or smell even a hint of smoke. He paused just inside the ground-floor exit. Thankfully, sirens wailed faintly in the distance just then and every head turned to watch for the approach of the fire trucks. He used the moment to slip outside with Shannon. They blended into the crowd of nervous neighbors.

Shannon said Lucifer was tall, well over six feet. He scanned the crowd for tall figures, examining each face carefully. None of them even remotely matched the pictures of Lucifer that H.O.T. Watch had sent him a few hours ago.

"I don't see him," Jake murmured to her. "Can I go back and do my job now?"

Regret and gratitude flickered in her gaze. "I'm sorry," she murmured.

He took a step away, but her hand shot out to grab his arm tightly. "Do you have to leave?"

He glanced nervously at the fire trucks starting to pull up. Any second, the building would be crawling with firemen. It was now or never. He glanced down at her and was riveted by the terror shining dully in her blue gaze. She really was scared. In the flashing red lights of the fire trucks she was as pale as a sheet. He glanced at the building behind him. Firemen were running into the lobby, axes over their shoulders. Dammit. He'd waited too long. He'd never make it past all those men and back into Shannon's place undetected.

His cell phone vibrated. Exasperated, he pulled it out and jammed it to his ear. "Go ahead."

"Boudreaux here. We just lost all the feeds from your cameras. Last video I have shows people racing out of the building like it's on fire. Say your status."

Jake winced. Someone had gotten into her place, found his equipment, and disabled it. He was screwed. Hell, the op was screwed. "I'm okay. Fire alarm went off. Had to evacuate with my hostess. Status of my gear unknown. Sounds like it was sabotaged, though."

Carter swore in his ear. "Hathaway's gonna kill you."

"The girl panicked. I had no choice."

"What are you going to do now?"

"See if I can spot whoever broke into her place. And then do damage control. What's going on at your end?"

Carter answered, "Our expert on the local movers and shakers in St. George just arrived. She's looking at the photos you sent now."

"She?" Jake asked in surprise.

"Yeah. Carina Rodriguez."

"Eduardo's daughter?"

"Yup. Although she'd tear your eyeballs out if she heard you describe her that way. She prefers to be called Joe Rodriguez's wife."

Jake grinned. Carina always had been a firecracker. "Give her my best. Is Joe with her?"

"Nah. He's en route to you."

Praise the Lord. *That* was good news. "Hey, Boo. I gotta run. Looks like the fire department's gonna start letting people back into the building." Jake hung up, his spirits buoyed by the news that his old comrade was going to come help him out down here. The backup would be a boon.

"C'mon, Shannon. I need to have a look at everyone as they head back inside."

"Why?" she asked as he dragged her to the front of the crowd.

"Just humor me." It was a long shot to think he could spot a Ferrare operative in this mob, but maybe he'd get lucky. He'd studied every picture of every known Ferrare associate long and hard before he'd come down here.

The fire chief was just waving to the crowd to indicate that they could return to their homes when a large, latté-skinned man barged through the crowd to loom in front of them. Jake tensed. Then facial identification kicked in. Not Lucifer.

"Shannon McMahon. You've been holding out on me, you minx!"

The second the man opened his mouth, Jake recognized

the voice. Octavius. The nosy neighbor from across the hall who fit the M.O. of a Ferrare informant.

"Good Lord, girlfriend, he's pretty. Where *did* you find him?"

Jake suppressed an urge to squirm as Octavius looked him up and down in frank admiration.

Shannon giggled nervously. "This is Jake. Jake Harrington. We, uhh, met online. I, uhh, tutor his nephew over the Internet."

"How very convenient," Octavius crooned. "And what brought him down here to this out-of-the-way spot all unannounced?"

Shannon looked about ready to throw up, so Jake dived in. "That's my fault. I had business in Venezuela and thought it would be fun to swing through here and meet her in person."

Octavius looked back and forth between them shrewdly.

Jake studied the man back. Interesting that the guy was fully dressed at this hour of the night. Just about everyone out here was wearing some combination of pajamas, robes and mismatched clothing. But Octavius was wearing a white dress shirt, dark slacks, shoes and socks, even a belt. Jake glanced down again at the man's trousers.

His gut clenched in sudden tension. He smiled pleasantly at Octavius and held out his hand. "You must be the famous best friend, Octavius. I've heard a lot about you."

Shannon's jaw was hanging slack, and she stared at him like he'd grown horns on his head. Dammit, she had to get with the program here or she'd give them away. Jake reached out awkwardly with his left hand—Octavius was still clutching his right hand—and wrapped it around Shannon's shoulder to drag her close.

"We were planning to call you tomorrow. Invite you over

for dinner. I just had to meet the man who told Brad Pitt how to dress properly."

Octavius finally let go of Jake's hand to wave his own negligently. "Boy was entirely underdressed for the night life in Rio. I can't believe Angie let him out of the hotel looking like that. That woman's got to take better care of her man, I tell you."

"Well, hey, Octavius. It looks like the fire department's letting us go back inside. It was nice meeting you. Let's get together tomorrow—well, later today at a civilized hour. I'd love to hear more."

Jake guided Shannon away from her gushing neighbor and inside. When they reached her apartment, he went over to the armoire immediately. As he'd suspected. All the wires were pulled out of the back of the cabinet, their exposed ends lying haphazardly on the floor.

He ordered quietly, "Go get dressed, Shannon. Grab your toothbrush and any medications you need."

"Huh?" she asked. He moved into the kitchen quickly, grabbing bottles of water, several tubes of crackers he'd spotted earlier and the big butcher knife out of a drawer. He tossed them into a small backpack he pulled out of his large duffel bag.

Shannon still hadn't moved. He glanced up at her impatiently. "What?"

"Tell me what's going on," she demanded.

"Octavius is an informant for Ferrare, and he was in here while you and I were outside. He sabotaged my gear. In about five minutes, Ferrare's men are going to arrive here to kidnap or kill us."

"How do you know all that?" Shannon exclaimed.

"The shins of Octavius's trousers were covered in white cat hair. Exactly the same way mine were after I crawled around on your floor setting up my equipment. Unless he owns Mignette's twin, he was in here."

Shannon still just stared at him.

"Get moving," he barked.

"Where are we going?"

"Away from here."

"But I don't want to leave," she responded in confusion. He sighed. Shock. He knew the signs well.

"You'll die if you stay. Ferrare's on to us, or he will be in the next few minutes. At best he'll kill you. At worst, he'll torture you to find out what you know and then kill you."

Shannon went dead pale. At least she believed him now. He continued sorting his gear urgently, separating out the weapons and things he had to take with him from the stuff he could afford to leave behind.

"If you don't move right now, you're going to have to leave with me in that nightgown."

"You can't mean it."

Frustrated, he dropped his bags, strode over to her and grabbed her by the upper arm, dragging her into her bedroom and over to her closet. He threw the door open, turned on the light, and grabbed a pair of jeans and a dark blue T-shirt. He took a bra and panties out of the baskets on a vertical shelf and threw them all at her. "Put these on, or I'll rip your nightgown off and put them on you myself."

Finally, she snapped out of her state of shock. "Go away," she mumbled as she pulled on the panties then dragged her jeans up under her gown.

"Hurry."

He figured they had about sixty more seconds before they had to rock and roll. He returned to the living room, finished sorting his gear, unlocked the cabinet and tossed the duffel he was leaving behind inside. He snapped the padlock shut again. No sense making Ferrare's job easier than it had to be.

It would take his men a few minutes to scare up an axe and bust into the cabinet. And Jake had a sinking feeling that every second was going to count if they were going to get away from here in one piece.

Chapter 12

Shannon shouldered the rucksack Jake handed her without complaint. After all, he was carrying a bulky bag about six times the size of hers, and it looked heavy. He grabbed Mignette's carrier and hurried out into the hall, pausing only long enough to lock her door and dead bolts from the outside. She was surprised when he headed for a stairwell instead of an elevator, though.

"Ferrare's men will ride up the elevators," he bit out in response to her questioning look.

She nodded and followed him out into the night. She was scared out of her mind at the prospect of mobsters invading her home, but at the same time she was relieved that Jake was with her. He knew what to do. He'd keep her safe. It was a strange feeling handing over responsibility for her safety to someone else. It was a nice change from the past seven years of constant fear.

"Can you run?" Jake asked.

"Uhh, sure. For a little while, at any rate."

He took off at what was probably a baby jog for him but was a stiff enough pace to make her huff and puff in a minute or two. They ran for ten minutes before the stitch in her side got so sharp she had to gasp, "I've got to stop for a minute and catch my breath."

Jake nodded tersely and dropped back to a walk. She really could've gone for a complete halt to bend over and gasp like she was dying for a while. But she supposed it was vital that they keep moving. Jake had led them into the old-town section of St. George. The city was divided into two parts, one a modern city laid out on a grid of streets at neat right angles. But the old town followed the contours of the hilly coast, twisting and turning in a narrow maze that often confounded even natives of the city.

"Where are we going?" she panted.

He shrugged. "Nowhere, yet. Once morning comes, we'll stash the cat somewhere and find a hidey hole."

"We're getting rid of Mignette?" she cried in dismay.

"Have you got a veterinarian or kennel or someplace similar where we can put her for a few days?"

"My veterinarian boards cats."

"Perfect. What time does the office open?"

"Nine o'clock, I think."

He nodded, then pulled out his cell phone. She listened as he murmured, "Yeah, I'm on the move. The hide got blown. I've got Shannon with me. We need to go to ground until morning. Any suggestions?"

He listened intently, then hung up without saying anything more.

"Well?" she demanded.

He glanced up at her, surprised. "My people have a safe house a couple of miles from here."

"Cool."

"Now we just have to get there without being followed."

Followed? Holy smokes! She looked back over her shoulder quickly.

"Okay. So, Shannon, when I tell you we're being followed, you've got to control that reflex to turn around and look. It'll get us killed if you do it when we actually are being followed."

She frowned. "Then we're not being followed?"

"Not yet. I was just testing you."

She scowled at him. "And I flunked?"

A ghost of a smile drifted across his otherwise grim features. "Pretty much."

She stuck her tongue out at him. They walked for a long time in silence. Three o'clock came and went, and still they walked. Exhaustion dragged at her feet, and her legs felt like lead. But she resisted the urge to ask when they were going to be there. She wasn't some whiny kid. She fully understood the stakes. And besides, Jake seemed completely focused on watching all around them for any sign of Ferrare's men. She didn't want to distract him.

Eventually, he seemed to relax. She ventured to ask, "Why did those men come into my apartment?"

"The guy who tried to mug you reported in to Ferrare that you had a friend who was more competent in a fight than the average bear. It aroused his suspicions. Then, when the first guy they sent in didn't come out with a report on what he found, they sent in Octavius. He must've spotted my surveillance gear."

"Too bad you didn't see Ferrare before all heck broke loose."

"Ahh, but I did," Jake murmured under his breath.

"Really? That's great news! You got the job done before they spotted you."

"Unfortunately, they spotted me back. Which means you

and I both are in deep doo-doo as long as we're within reach of Ferrare's men."

That silenced her. So much for starting to relax a little. Tense and nervous once more, she followed him ever deeper into the maze of ancient streets.

Finally, he ducked into an early 1800's vintage stone building. He pulled her back into the deep shadows of the vestibule and then stood just inside the door for a long time, staring out into the night. Eventually, he seemed satisfied and nodded at her to proceed up the stairs. By the time she reached the fourth floor, Shannon was certain her legs were going to collapse.

"This way," he murmured, leading her down a short hallway to a door with old brass numbers nailed to it announcing it to be unit forty-two. He knocked quietly on the door.

She fidgeted while they waited for an answer, which seemed to take an inordinately long time. She was about to suggest to him that he knock again when the door opened a crack. Jake gave some sort of complicated hand signal, and whoever was inside nodded. The door closed, a chain rattled, then the door opened fully. Jake slipped inside, and she followed close on his heels.

Their host said nothing, but merely averted his eyes, slipped out into the hall and pulled the door closed behind him.

"He's leaving?" Shannon asked in surprise.

Jake nodded. "The less he knows, the better for all of us, including him."

Ahh. That must've been why the guy didn't even glance at her. Didn't want to know what she looked like in case anyone asked.

Jake slid his pack off his shoulders and set Mignette's carrier down. "We can crash here until we figure out what we're going to do next."

"Isn't it obvious?" she replied. "We're going to leave the country on the first plane tomorrow morning."

He shrugged. "You're leaving. But my mission's not finished."

"I thought you were supposed to identify Ferrare. And you already did that."

He sighed. "That was only part of the job."

When he didn't elaborate, she prompted, "And the other part was…?"

"To figure out what the guy's up to, and then kill him."

Kill—of course. She should've expected that.

Jake was talking again. "When a man like him starts having secret meetings with people arriving in limousines in the middle of the night, he's up to something big. And it can't possibly be good."

"How do you plan to proceed?" she asked curiously. It seemed to her like Ferrare had the upper hand. This was his town, and he'd just managed to chase off the American government's best shot at watching him.

"The less you know, the better at this point," Jake answered stiffly.

She supposed he had a point, but she always had been too curious for her own good. She tapped a front tooth with her fingernail. "If I were you, I'd get a disguise and head back to that area. Someone on the street is bound to know something. The guy's got maids and cooks and drivers, and one of them will talk. A family member will tell another family member, who'll tell a close friend, who tells another, and before long everyone in the neighborhood will know what he's up to."

Jake frowned. "A man like Ferrare insists fanatically on loyalty—and silence—from his employees. He's been known to threaten to kill his people's families if anyone talks."

Shannon shuddered. Nasty guy. She wandered through the tiny living room and into what appeared to be the only bedroom. A narrow double bed took most of the space. She jumped when Jake spoke from just behind her. "Why don't you lie down and get a little rest? You must be exhausted after I dragged you halfway across town on foot."

She glanced over her shoulder. "What about you? Aren't you tired?"

He shrugged. "I'll keep watch."

"I thought this place was a safe house. Emphasis on safe."

"Just being cautious."

She snorted. "Yeah, well, even superheroes have to sleep. You take the bed. I already got a few hours of sleep tonight, and I'm a lot shorter than you. I'll take the couch."

He gave her a withering look. "What kind of cad do you take me for? The lady gets the bed."

She glared. "Are you going to stand there arguing with me all night long?"

"If I have to," he answered evenly.

"Are you always this stubborn?" she demanded.

"Absolutely. Get used to it."

A warm feeling fluttered through her. She could get very used to him, indeed, given half a chance. "How 'bout we share the bed?"

"Oh, no," he answered sharply. "I'm not going there."

"Why not? You were willing to go there a few hours ago."

"And that was a mistake."

Her gaze narrowed. "If you think I'm going to turn tail and slink away like a kicked puppy, you've got another think coming, mister."

Definite alarm blossomed in his gaze.

She continued, "If you recall, I was there for that kiss, too. I felt the way you reacted to me. You wanted me as much as I wanted you. Don't even bother trying to deny it."

"Like I said. It was a mistake." She thought she heard a note of desperation in his voice.

"If that kiss was a mistake, then I'm the Easter Bunny."

"Why don't you hop on into the bedroom, Bun, because this conversation is over."

Fine. He didn't want to talk anymore? She could handle that. She took a step toward him, and his eyes popped open wide. Oh, yeah. He saw it coming.

"You are the stubbornest—" she took another step forward "orneriest—" another step "—most cussed, exasperating man—" one final step put her practically chest to chest with him "—I've ever met."

His throat bobbed as he gulped.

She looked up at him. "Kiss me, you idiot."

"Uhh, Shannon, I don't think that's such a great idea—"

She cut him off. "Fine. If you're too chicken to do it, I will." She reached up on tiptoe and looped her arms around his neck, tugging his head down to her. She noted that he didn't put up much of a fight for a man who could break her in half at the drop of a hat. Uh-huh. That's what she thought.

Her mouth touched his. His lips were warm and firm and resilient. And he seemed determined not to participate in this kiss. Without breaking their mouth-to-mouth contact, she grinned and murmured, "You realize it's completely childish to try to hold out on me, right?"

"Yeah," he muttered back, "but it's the right thing to do."

She pressed her entire body against his and gasped at the sensation. "Sorry, but I have to disagree. *This* is right." She intentionally overbalanced forward so Jake was forced to take a stumbling step. His arms grabbed her reflexively.

"Better," she purred.

He glared down at her. "This is assault, you know."

She laughed aloud. "Oh, please let me be there when you stand in front of the judge and try to explain how the weak, little, five-foot-three teacher picked on the big, bad military sniper who's trained to kill with his bare hands."

He scowled. "Yeah, but I can't hurt you. None of my combat skills count."

"You're right. This is a battle of the sexes." Her thrill at being in his arms clouded for a moment at the memory of Lucifer's face. She continued more seriously, "Barring sexual predators who don't actually count for sex because they're really about violence and power, women always win the battle of the sexes, you know."

His arms tightened at the reference to her previous attack. "Your past is all the more reason for us not to do this."

She sighed. "I've had years of counseling. It's not something you ever get over, but you do learn to move beyond it. I've just never found the right guy to move beyond it with. Until now. But I'm not a head case."

"You won't know that until you actually have, uhh, a relationship with a guy again," he objected.

"Fair enough. So let's give it a go."

He huffed. "I don't want to be the one responsible for… rehabbing you."

Okay. That stung. His arms began to loosen, and she felt him drawing away from her emotionally. And then it hit her. He'd taken that jab with the intention of pushing her away from him. Why would he do—of course.

She reached up and laid her palm against his cheek. Razor stubble was rough against her hand, but the skin beneath was smooth and warm. Like the man himself. "Jake," she sighed. "Why do you keep running away from all contact with the human race? You're a good man. There's no reason to punish yourself like this."

Something angry, denial maybe, flared in his eyes, tarnishing their silver surface until it was dark and opaque.

Trepidation wobbled in her stomach, but she took a steadying breath, reached up, and kissed him again.

He didn't stay passive beneath her touch for long this time. In fact, he swept her up against him with a growl under his breath and kissed her back. Forcefully. Almost as if he was trying to scare her off. And maybe that would've worked when he first showed up on her doorstep. But she knew him better now. Had utter confidence in his self-control. *Trusted* him.

"You are so hosed," she murmured.

His head jerked up enough for him to demand, "Why?"

"Because I'm so not buying that bad-boy act."

He swore foully under his breath, and she laughed in return. Yup. She'd pegged him spot on. "Give up, already, Jake. I'm getting in your pants, and there's nothing you can do about it except give in gracefully."

"I cannot believe this is happening. The guy is the one who's supposed to come on to the girl."

Shannon shrugged. "I want this. I need this. I need *you*."

"But I *don't* want it," he retorted.

She kissed her way up the column of his neck and paused in the vicinity of his ear. "But," she whispered, "you do want me."

Jake moved abruptly, sweeping her off her feet and swinging her up into his arms. He strode into the bedroom and dropped her onto what turned out to be a thin and lumpy mattress with squeaky springs. He glared down at her as he stripped his shirt off over his head and jerked at his belt buckle.

She stared up at him, transfixed. She'd won. For better or worse, she'd breached his defenses. A moment's doubt assailed her at the demons she would find inside his fortress of solitude, but she pushed the thought aside. She could do this. They could do this.

His gaze was black as he reached for her T-shirt and yanked

it over her head. "Take off your pants," he ordered. His voice was grim. Focused. Furious.

She ought to be scared out of her mind. But she just couldn't summon anything in herself except profound relief that the moment had finally come to resume living like a normal human being. Now. If only she could do the same for him.

His body was beautiful. It was scarred and hard and as unyielding as the man himself. But all that honed power screamed of safety to her. Of protection. Of being cared for.

Clearly, she had entered some sort of delusional state, for she ought to be running from this guy for all she was worth. But just as clearly, he'd cast a spell over her. And she wasn't about to break it.

"Are you sure about this?" he rasped.

She nodded.

"Say it out loud. I don't want there to be any room for recriminations later. Tell me you want me to make love to you."

He sounded like he was about to execute a contract to kill a man. She gulped. "I want you to…to make love to me, Jake. Now."

He nodded tersely as if acknowledging an order.

"Do you have to be so military about this?" she asked hesitantly. "Can you maybe relax a little?"

He gave a short bark of what passed for laughter, but the strain in his voice was too extreme to be sure. She'd stopped undressing at her underwear, but Jake reached for her bra. It had a convenient front clasp, and he hooked a finger under it and popped it open, spilling her breasts into his hands.

"Nice," he commented as calmly as if he were remarking on the weather.

"Nice?" she repeated in mock indignation. "Women prefer it if you groan in ecstasy and say something more along the lines of 'Damn, those knockers are perfect.'"

His gaze jerked up to hers.

"Lighten up, Jake. You're supposed to enjoy this."

He scowled. "I don't need instruction from you, thanks."

She laughed. "Well, then, by all means get on with it, maestro."

"It's a good thing I'm confident with my sexual prowess, or that mouth of yours would ruin the mood."

"Then do something with my mouth to keep it busy," she murmured.

That finally got a laugh out of him and a flash of those killer dimples. Better. His gaze was warm and shining as he closed the distance between them and kissed her. This time his mouth was slow and thorough against hers. His hand slid down her thigh, and she realized belatedly that he'd neatly divested her of her panties. Okay, give the guy points for smooth moves.

"If you want to stop at any time, Shannon...."

"I'll let you know, and you'll stop. And now that the public-service announcement is concluded—"

He cut her off, laughing against her lips. "You talk too much."

And then he stole her breath away with his hands and mouth until she couldn't talk at all.

Chapter 13

Jake's entire being shuddered with need. This woman was a fire that burned him up from the inside out. He wanted her worse than life. But deep within him another voice screamed at him, denying her, denying him. He didn't deserve this! He was not supposed to connect with other human beings. Not supposed to find pleasure. Not supposed to fall for a beautiful woman and make passionate love with her. He was a *monster*.

Here was a woman who'd been brutalized and assaulted, and he was supposed to be her first after that? He was no better than her attacker. Hell, he was a whole lot worse. He rolled away from her in self-disgust.

"I swear. You're worse than a forty-year-old virgin, Jake."

A virgin? He was a lot of things, but anything pertaining to innocence was not one of them. He laughed. He couldn't help it. The woman simply did not get who or what he was.

And maybe that was the key to her appeal. She was so damned naive at the end of the day. She'd been exposed to the worst that mankind had to offer, and she still had faith in her fellow man. She still believed that happiness was possible. Yeah, she was afraid—she wasn't stupid, after all—but she still had guts enough to go for what she wanted when she found it.

"You're a hell of a woman."

"Care to show me that instead of just talking about it?"

"You don't give up, do you?"

"Nope. I never gave up when Lucifer had me tied to my bed and I was half-dead, and I'm sure as heck not giving up on you when we're both lying here of our own free will and turned on."

He closed his eyes. "For the last time, this isn't right."

"And for the last time, you're full of sh—"

He rolled over and cut her off, kissing her hard. The bed springs screeched.

She giggled. "Oh my gosh, this is going to be loud."

"You have no idea, darlin'."

Apparently, he'd surrendered. His face was buried between her breasts and his hand was buried between her legs and she was sweet and hot around him. And the last thing on his mind was stopping this insanity.

He should've been gentle. Taken it slow. Eased her into the idea of making love again with caresses and romantic sweet-talking until she was lost in passion and begging for more.

But he didn't have it in him. He wasn't a gentle man. Hadn't been raised like that and had never learned it along the way. He only knew how to follow his instincts, to ride the wave of lust pounding between them. To be raw and honest and play no games.

She danced upon his fingers, bathing them with the evidence of her need, while she thrust her breasts up into his mouth for more attention there, too. "Harder," she gasped.

He obliged, and she moaned her pleasure. "Open your legs," he ordered.

Her thighs fell apart, and he took full advantage of her vulnerable position to drive both of them closer to the edge of the cliff looming before them.

"Mmm. That feels good," she purred as he stroked more moisture from her body. His own body reacted, jumping sharply at the thought of burying himself in her.

"Please, Jake?"

"Ahh. The lady knows how to beg, does she?"

Shannon tensed briefly, then relaxed. Intuition told him he'd accidentally crossed a Lucifer boundary. But when she reached for his male flesh, quickly sheathed him in a condom and then guided him toward her, he released the breath he'd been holding. "Grab the headboard, darlin'. You're going to need it."

Again she tensed, and again she relaxed. He waited until she sprawled wantonly in front of him, her gaze fixed on his, the only tension in her body eager anticipation.

"Last chance to change your mind," he murmured.

"You talk too much," she retorted.

Grinning, he moved forward. Guided his male flesh to her female opening. He paused for a moment, giving her one last, unspoken chance to back out. When she moaned softly in nothing but need he surged forward, sheathing himself to the hilt in her hot, wet body. Her internal muscles clenched him so tightly he thought he might pass out.

"You okay?" he ground out, doing his damnedest to stay still and not slam into her mindlessly.

"I forgot," she breathed. "That feels incredible."

"Now, that's an understatement," he mumbled. He moved experimentally, easing back and then gliding forward again.

She threw her head back and cried out.

He did it again.

Again she cried out. "More, Jake. Oh, please. More."

He covered her fists with his, wrapping his fingers around the narrow spindle of the headboard she gripped convulsively. Thus anchored to her and to reality, he let go of everything else, pumping into her slowly at first and then with increasing speed and force. The bed squeaked like it was going to come apart, the headboard banged rhythmically against the wall and Shannon moaned and sighed and eventually shouted.

And all the while, he was consumed by a pleasure so deliriously overwhelming that the entire world ceased to exist. It was just him and Shannon. Together. Alive. Driving each other completely out of their minds. And not a damned thing else mattered.

His shout rose to mingle with hers as his orgasm exploded so hard he momentarily went blind with the power of it. He didn't exactly pass out, but he came damned close. Shannon sagged beneath him, her body slick with perspiration. Her fingers went slack beneath his, but he didn't let them go.

"Wow," she breathed.

"Who says I'm done with you yet?" he murmured.

She jolted, then went as soft as a down comforter beneath him again. Her glorious eyes fluttered open. He didn't allow himself women often—hardly ever, in fact—but tonight he planned to take complete advantage of the moment. His body was already growing hard again inside her.

"Oh. Oh, my," she murmured.

She was already undulating beneath him again, her body rising to his, coaxing him into that other place of mindless, blinding pleasure. He took his time this time, stroking her body to orgasm after orgasm until she quivered around him in exhaustion.

"I can't take any more," she gasped.

"Ahh, but you can. You're the strongest woman I've ever met." He didn't relent but continued driving into her until she cried out again, a keening wail of raw pleasure torn from the depths of her soul. The sound of it sent him over the edge into his own release, every bit as intense as the first one but perhaps even more galvanizing to his soul. Shannon gazed up at him in naked hero worship, panting.

"More?" he asked.

Disbelief vibrated in her voice. "Seriously?"

"I wouldn't have asked if I didn't mean it."

"You're hard on your women, Jake."

He laughed quietly. "Are you complaining?"

"Not in the least. I just had no idea you were so…fit."

That curved his mouth up into a grin. "It's the company I keep."

She smiled, and it pierced him all the way to the soul. She was everything a woman was meant to be and more: gentle, passionate, giving and powerful. A goddess. And she'd opened her heart and her body to him. All he could do was worship at the altar of her big blue eyes, losing himself in her divinity, drinking in every drop of her essence she deigned to share with him.

He slid down her body slowly, kissing and caressing every glorious inch of her. He learned every curve, every angle, every ticklish spot, every silken length of sleek flesh. Her fingers slid through his hair, a benediction.

"Jake. What are you doing to me?"

"I'm trying to give you back a little of the same pleasure you've given me."

"I've died and gone to heaven."

He smiled against her belly and murmured, "My own personal angel."

He took his time this time, their lovemaking slow and lazy and gentle, maybe finally worthy of her. An aching sweetness unfolded inside him, totally foreign and yet so addictive he feared he'd never be the same again. He didn't know what it was, but he was powerless to resist it. It emanated from Shannon and sucked him in so completely, so thoroughly, that he felt as if he'd given away the greatest part of himself to her. And yet, he felt no loss. She'd given him something back, something that slipped so easily and neatly into the void in his soul that for the first time he could ever remember, he felt whole.

It was stunning.

And when she gazed up into his eyes, shattering before him into a climax that sent tears down her cheeks, he shattered as well. Completely. Into a million pieces he couldn't ever possibly put back together again. He was lost. All he could do was stare down at her and be amazed at what she'd done to him.

Eventually, her legs unwrapped limply from around his hips. "Uncle," she sighed with a smile.

He dropped a light kiss on her forehead and rolled to the side, gathering her close lest she feel as abandoned as he did at being separated from her body like this. He spoke quietly. "Sleep now."

She murmured drowsily, "You can stop giving me orders. I'm a civilian, thank you very much."

"As you wish. *Please* go to sleep now."

Her eyes closed and she snuggled against his side, her head on his shoulder. Her body went slack in about ten seconds. He eased his arm out from underneath her and swung his feet to the floor. Then he sat on the side of the bed, staring in disbelief at nothing.

What in the hell had just happened between them? He knew better than to jump in the sack with a principal in a mission. But damned if the woman hadn't seduced him...and he'd let her. And damned if that hadn't been the best sex he'd ever had. The kind of sex a guy wanted a hell of a lot more of.

Correction. That had been way more than sex. And he still wanted a hell of a lot more of it.

Except he knew better. Sex, relationships, women like Shannon—they were not for him. They simply didn't fit in with the rest of his life. His real life. The one where he stalked and killed people for a living.

She might have been able to put her demons behind her, but he wasn't so lucky. Plenty of demons still loomed in front of him. They had names. Faces. Families. And he'd killed them all.

He'd always known the job would turn on him someday. The shrinks had briefed all the sniper candidates on it thoroughly, had made them sign documents stating that they understood this job would screw them up in the heads and they were volunteering anyway.

But he'd never really believed the psychobabble bull. He'd grown up different from the other guys, been raised apart from regular people by a man who was a killer himself. He was immune to the usual bouts of social conscience and guilt. When a person had never been a part of society, he couldn't freak out at its loss, could he?

He glanced over his shoulder at Shannon. She looked like a dark angel lying there, her black hair spread out on the white pillows. God, she was beautiful.

He might not be able to lose what he'd never had…but he'd had her, now. He could lose her, now. And the idea scared the hell out of him. Bad enough that his hands were shaking and cold fear filled him up. *This* was why he held himself apart. Why he'd never joined the human race.

But she'd held his nose and forced it down his throat like bad-tasting medicine. And it had turned out to be delicious. Addictive. Not medicine at all. Manna from heaven. A connection he could wallow in forever. Certainty settled deep in his gut that it was going to kill him. She'd taken from him the one thing that had always been his edge—his detachment.

But he still had a mission to do.

He was going to fail. And hundreds or thousands of people would ultimately die because of it.

Shannon rolled over and startled awake at the feel of bare, cool sheets beside her. Where was Jake? She moved to sit up, to look for him, and her body protested. He'd used her hard, and she'd reveled in every minute of it. Thank God he hadn't pussyfooted around her like she was some fragile, breakable thing. If he had, she'd have become horribly self-conscious and potentially not been able to go through with it. Exultation erupted in her gut. But she had! She'd had sex again, and it had been wonderful! It was as if a giant, missing piece of her had just been handed back.

She spied Jake, naked, standing in the shadows by the window peering down at the street below. Lord, he was amazing to look at. And to think he was hers. Well, for now, at least. But maybe for longer. She felt a definite connection between them. He made her feel safe, and she made him laugh. That was a good base to build on, wasn't it?

"Hey, there, handsome," she called quietly. "Come back to bed?"

He glanced over at her, and she reeled back from the cold distance in his gaze. Wait, he was working. It was nothing personal. She'd interrupted him when he was concentrating on all that grim military stuff. He didn't answer aloud, which was a little weird. But then she thought back to when he'd first arrived at her apartment and he'd been pretty taciturn.

"Go back to sleep," he finally said in a clipped tone.

She rolled onto her side with her back to the faint light coming in through the window. He'd be in a better mood in the morning.

* * *

Except he wasn't. She could hardly get a word out of him at breakfast. They sat at a minuscule bistro table in the equally minuscule kitchen and split a stale baguette and a pot of bitter coffee between them. He pulled out a map of St. George after the silent meal and had her point out the exact location of her veterinarian's office. It was all the way across town from where he showed her they were now.

He reached for a phone book. "We need to find someplace closer to stash the cat."

She frowned. "Mignette is my pet. I love her like my child, and I won't trust her to just anybody."

"Oh, for crying out loud. She's a cat. Cats don't give a damn for humans. As long as they get fed and pampered, they don't care who does it."

Shannon's gaze narrowed. He was trying to pick a fight. But she wasn't rising to the bait. She replied reasonably, "Have you got a better idea than grabbing a taxi and going to my vet's office?"

"Yeah. Find a closer place. I don't want to expose us as much as it would if we rode in a cab."

"So we disguise ourselves."

"Easier said than done."

"Why don't you call that magic guy on your cell phone who seems to solve all your logistical problems with a wave of his hand?"

"You mean H.O.T. Watch?" he blurted, startled.

"Yeah, sure. Is that what the guy's called?"

"It's actually a whole staff of guys—and gals."

"So call them."

He shot her a disgusted look. "I can handle one spoiled house cat all by myself."

She shrugged. "Then why are you trying to turn this into an argument?"

He subsided at that, thumbing through the phone book in thick silence. After a minute or so, he said, "How about this place?" He pointed at a large advertisement in the business pages. "Based on the prices, I have to assume it's a pretty swanky kennel. It says they take cats, too. And it's only a few blocks from here."

She studied the ad dubiously. She supposed it was better than dumping Mignette on the street to fend for herself, and in Jake's current mood, she was sure the thought had crossed his mind. "Fine. We can always go have a look at it."

He stood up and fiddled with something on the counter. "Here. Put these in your purse." He held out a handful of toothpicks.

"What are those?"

"A disguise."

Ooo-kay. She pocketed the toothpicks without comment.

He was still muttering under his breath about having to deal with a damned cat when the two of them set out. They'd taken about ten steps down the now-crowded street when she heard his cell phone vibrating.

"Yeah?" he said into it. Then, "Thank you for telling me I'm on the move. I might have missed that if you hadn't."

Whoa. Feeling a little sarcastic this morning, was he? She was just glad it wasn't directed at her. Why was he so grouchy? He'd escaped from a dangerous situation last night and topped off the evening with great sex—and lots of it. At least it had been great sex for her. And judging from the noises he'd made last night, it hadn't been too shabby for him, either.

He listened to the phone in silence for a long time then muttered a quick "Later" and hung up. He didn't volunteer any information. Aware of the press of pedestrians around her, she didn't ask for any, either.

The boarding facility turned out to be new and modern, and in short order Mignette was installed in her own small room, complete with a human-sized be and a radio tuned to a station with music the cat was accustomed to hearing at home. An attendant was crooning over what a beautiful kitty she was when Jake unceremoniously grabbed Shannon's arm and dragged her out the door.

It felt strange being away from Minnie. It was as if her last tie to the past seven years had just been severed. She'd left everything she owned behind in her apartment, and now her constant companion was gone. An urge to cry washed over her.

"C'mon," Jake muttered, turning in the opposite direction from last night's safe house.

So much for the incredible sensitivity he'd shown her last night. She would never forget the final time they made love. She could've sworn those had been tears shining in his eyes by the end.

"Where are we going?" she asked, surprised. She'd assumed they'd go back to the crash pad and wait for further instructions about how to get the heck out of Dodge.

"To get wheels."

"I beg your pardon?"

He glanced over at her impatiently. "We need a van."

"Why?" she asked blankly.

"Not here," he bit out.

She glanced around. Nobody nearby seemed to be listening in any way to their low-voiced conversation. But if he didn't think it was safe to talk, so be it.

"Look sharp for police or military types. If you see any, tell me immediately."

He could really quit snapping out orders at her this morning. Nonetheless, she nodded her acknowledgment of the instructions. In the middle of a street was probably not the ideal place to tell him to get over his snit and start acting nice.

A police car rounded a corner up the hill from them and maybe two blocks away. Jake spotted it about the same time she did. He grabbed her arm and yanked her into the nearest store, a small market. Jeez. He was acting like they were dangerous fugitives. Was there something he wasn't telling her? Oh, wait. There was a whole lot he wasn't telling her at the moment.

"Browse the damned fruit," he bit out.

Obediently, she tested every mango in the crate before her for its ripeness. But rebellion simmered in her gut. When they got by themselves, he was darn well going to tell her what was up with him.

"And are we buying anything this morning?" she asked.

He was looking out the front window. The police car cruised past slowly. "No," he replied absently. "C'mon. We've got to get moving. The search for us will only get more intense as the day goes on."

"There's a search on for us?" she squeaked.

"Hush."

She gulped and followed him back onto the street. Instead of it being a warm, sunny morning rich with the promise of a new day, all of a sudden the Old Town was a menacing place. The buildings loomed gray and grim, their windows black like disapproving eyes topped by stony brows. Everyone on the street suddenly seemed to be looking at them, aware that strangers and criminals were in their midst.

Dread crept around her throat, a choking necklace, and she started to have trouble breathing as Jake maintained a brisk pace up a steep hill. "Can we slow down a little?" she panted.

He glanced over at her, surprise giving way to irritation. "You're hyperventilating. You have to keep breathing normally."

"Yeah, well, that's hard to do when everyone's looking at us."

"No one's looking at us. Not yet, at any rate. Although if you make much more of a spectacle of yourself, they will be."

"I'm sorry, but I happen to be an amateur at this stuff. I'm not a trained—"

He slapped a hand over her mouth before she could name him a killer aloud. Probably for the best. But it didn't do much to calm her agitation.

"Get a grip," he growled.

Right. No sweat. Just tell her most primitive fight-or-flight reflexes to take a five-minute break. "You're going to have to distract me."

He blinked, uncomprehending.

"Talk to me, Jake. About anything. Something stupid to take my mind off of…well, you know what."

"I don't exactly do inane conversation."

"Fine. Talk to me about something serious and significant. Like the price of tea in China."

An unwilling grin tried to crack his granite features but ultimately failed. He sighed. "Did you know that Old Town in St. George is one of the oldest European settlements in South America? Spanish and Portuguese traders sailed here and established a port not long after North America was first settled."

She turned and started walking up the hill.

He continued, "I hear the Opera House is one of the finest small theaters in the world."

She nodded. "I've been there. The acoustics are phenomenal."

"What performance did you see?"

"*Carmen.*" She threw him a sidelong glance. "You know.

The one about the brazen hussy who seduces the man of her dreams."

He looked ahead stonily, not rising to that bait.

The tactic worked. Her breathing calmed down and the panic receded to a dim vibration in the back of her mind, present and waiting to reemerge but quiescent for now.

The crowd thinned as they left the commercial district and passed into a residential area. She leaned close to him and murmured, "Care to tell me what we're going to do with the van once we've got one?"

"We're going to pick up some friends of mine. And then we're going to finish this thing once and for all."

She reeled back. Was he only talking about finishing the mission? Or was he talking about more than that? About finishing this thing between him and her once and for all? She prayed it was the former. But she feared it was the latter.

Chapter 14

Shannon shifted in the cold sand. They lay on a deserted beach that gleamed dully under a sliver of waning moonlight. Something sharp poked her hip. One of Jake's toothpicks.

She'd been stunned when they walked into a used-car lot to hear him speak in fluent Spanish around a toothpick that hung out the corner of his mouth in open defiance of gravity. She hadn't believed a single toothpick could be an entire disguise, but the car salesman hadn't been able to take his eyes off that sliver of wood. Jake had negotiated to buy a van, paid the guy with a credit card from a local Gavronese bank and collected the keys without the man ever seeming to look directly into Jake's eyes.

She reached into her pocket and moved the toothpick so it wouldn't poke her. "Where did you learn to speak Spanish so well?" she asked, breaking the silence between them.

He didn't bother to glance over at her but continued to gaze out to sea through a hand-held gadget that looked like half of a pair of binoculars. "Defense Language Institute."

She frowned. Why, after last night's spectacular lovemaking with her, was he treating her like this? She'd tried to ask him a couple of times already, and he'd either ducked the question or simply refused outright to talk about it. If she weren't so dead certain that last night had affected him as much as it had affected her, she could've started taking his rejection act a little personally. She sighed. Okay, so she was taking it way personally. She hadn't had real sex in almost a decade, and the day after her first foray back into the world of the sexually active, her lover was acting like she was a leper. Who wouldn't take that personally?

"Jake—"

He waved a sharp hand, cutting her off.

"What?" she snapped irritably.

"I've got movement."

"You're looking at the ocean. It's probably some pompano jumping out of the water. Or maybe you just saw a wave breaking."

His jaw rippled. "I know what fish and waves look like, thank you."

Her own irritation mounted. But it did give her an idea. Maybe she could needle him into talking to her. Lord knew, gentle understanding and long-suffering patience hadn't done a thing to dent his fortress of solitude.

"So, tell me. We're sitting on a cold beach in the middle of the night in front of some burned-out ruin staring at the ocean *why?*"

"I told you. We're meeting some friends of mine."

"Oh. That's right. I forgot. You speak to mermaids."

Inexplicably, a grin flickered across his face. "I'll be sure to tell the guys you think they're mermaids."

"Whatever." She glanced around the deserted stretch of beach. "What is this place, anyway?"

Thankfully, he answered. She was getting pretty desperate

for him to talk to her about anything at all. "This estate used to be owned by Eduardo Ferrare. He owned nearly a mile of beachfront, and that black hole behind us used to be the mansion he ran his drug empire out of."

Intrigued, she commented, "I didn't peg you for the kind of person who felt a compulsion to return to the scene of the crime."

He shrugged. "Funny thing, but this is the only stretch of beach on the entire coastline that has no radar coverage by the Gavronese Coast Guard."

"Did Ferrare arrange that, you think?"

Jake glanced over at her, his eyes twin chips of ice. "Of course he did. He no doubt ran shipments of drugs out of here along with his various other smuggling activities. There's deep water until about a hundred feet from shore at this spot we're sitting."

"How did you stop him?"

"We infiltrated one of our guys into the house by having him marry Eduardo's daughter Carina and eventually took the operation down from the inside."

"And Ferrare's daughter went along with that?" Shannon exclaimed.

"She was a prisoner in the place and knew her old man for the monster he was. She was all over helping us stop her father. She ended up staying married to our guy. They're crazy in love."

Shannon looked around with fresh eyes. The blackened area behind her was huge. "That must've been some mansion."

"It was impressive. Quite the display of drug-funded, ostentatious excess."

"So why are we here tonight, if it's not to reminisce about the good old days?"

"I told you. To meet some friends."

"What? Are they just going to rise up out of the ocean?"

"Something like that."

She frowned. Silence settled around them once more, but it wasn't quite as brittle as before. At least not for a minute or two. Then it was as if it had occurred to Jake that he'd let down his guard. All of a sudden, his body went tense. He emotionally withdrew from her as surely as if he'd physically sidled away from her.

"What are you thinking right now?" she blurted. She knew he wouldn't answer, but she couldn't help asking.

"I'm thinking you need to be quiet so I can concentrate on doing my job."

She swore under her breath. She couldn't exactly argue against that. He did have an important and dangerous job, and it would be wrong of her to interfere with it. Frustrated, she hugged her knees and tried to stay warm in the face of his chill and the night's cold.

After a little while, Jake fished in his bag and pulled out a handful of wires. He deftly untangled them and donned some sort of necklace thingie that looked like a microphone pressed against his throat. He inserted an earpiece into his right ear.

Then, a few minutes later, he touched his throat and murmured, "Tallyho."

What? Were they foxhunting now? She looked around, confused.

"Roger. Come ten degrees right."

"Who on earth are you talking to?" she demanded.

"My friends."

"The ones who are going to rise up from the sea?"

"Yeah."

Dang it. He'd gone all silent and distant again. The guy was giving her whiplash with this hot-and-cold act of his. She started as something did rise up from the sea. A dark, vaguely humanoid form. Several of them, in fact. And then a couple more. She counted five in all. What the—

"All clear to come ashore," Jake murmured.

In a matter of seconds, five men waded ashore, stripped off wet suits and stood before her and Jake in dark street clothes with backpacks like Jake's slung over their shoulders. They were big and strong and exuded the same self-contained confidence that Jake did.

"Wow. You are the ugliest mermaids I've ever seen," she remarked lightly.

"Uhh, thanks, I think," one of them said, grinning. He was a dark-haired man who looked to be in his late thirties. The other men seemed to be deferring to him a little, like he was the leader. "My name's Tom. You must be Miss McMahon."

The warmth in his voice stood in stark contrast to the cold shoulder Jake had been giving her. She smiled up at this man gratefully. "Call me Shannon."

"Shannon, these ugly mermaids are Tex, Dutch, Mac and Doc."

She nodded politely. "It's nice to meet you. Although I have to say I never knew mermaids had such strange names."

Tom grinned. "Those are our field handles—our nicknames. They'll probably be easier to remember than my men's real names. My handle's Hoss, if you must know. But feel free to just call me Tom."

She glanced over at Jake. "What's his nickname? Lurch?"

Low chuckles erupted all around. The one called Doc replied, "Nah. We call him Howdy. In honor of what a friendly and outgoing guy he is."

"Riigghhtt," she drawled.

Dutch slapped Jake on the shoulder. "I see she's already intimately familiar with your sparkling personality, bro."

Heat leaped to her cheeks. Thank goodness it was pitch dark out here and they couldn't see her blush. She felt Jake tense briefly beside her, but then he relaxed once more. He murmured, "The van's this way. Did Ops find us a safe house, or are we on our own?"

Tom rattled off an address she was unfamiliar with. Jake nodded, however. When did he get to know St. George so well? Even natives got lost in this town on a routine basis.

The men strode down the beach fast enough that she had to all but jog to keep up. Jake was the shortest one of the bunch, and he was nearly six feet tall. Sometimes it stunk being five foot three, and this was one of those times. Thankfully, the van wasn't far away. The men slipped inside the windowless back of the vehicle, and she was surprised to see that they seemed to expect her to take the front passenger's seat.

Jake slipped behind the wheel. He pulled away from the beach and guided the van through the beachside tourist strip of restaurants and souvenir shops toward the city proper.

"Why am I sitting up here?" she murmured to him.

"Cover."

"Huh?"

"You're acting as a cover. If anyone sees a woman sitting in this van, they won't think it's a suspicious or possibly dangerous vehicle."

Great. Now she'd been relegated to the status of a toothpick.

Tom spoke from the shadows in the back. "Carina has ID'd the men who came to visit Ferrare last night."

"Carina Ferrare?" Shannon blurted.

Doc spoke up wryly. "Carina Rodriguez, now. My wife."

Ahh. So he was the one who'd gone into Ferrare's stronghold

undercover. She peered at him, trying to make out his features more clearly. Brave guy.

Jake interrupted her train of thought. "And who were they?"

Tom replied, "Two of Gavarone's top three military generals."

"And the fourth guy's the one who went missing after he came to visit Eduardo?" Jake asked.

"That's correct," Tom answered.

"H.O.T. Watch got any guesses as to what's going on?"

"They speculate that a coup d'état may be in the offing."

The van jerked to the right slightly, and then Jake corrected course. "No kidding?" he asked.

"Nope."

Shannon turned in her seat and stared over her shoulder. Things hadn't ever really settled down in Gavarone since the civil war five years ago. But a military takeover of the government? That one she hadn't seen coming.

Tom continued. "The intel guys believe that Eduardo may be financing the junta the same way he financed the rebels in the civil war."

Whoa. Shannon had never heard a hint of any drug lord's involvement in the rebel movement that had torn the country apart.

Jake's jaw was noticeably tight when he asked, "What's our mission?"

"Determine if a coup's about to happen and stop it if it does."

"Eduardo?" Jake bit out.

"He's fair game."

Shannon couldn't help herself. She asked incredulously, "You six guys are supposed to stop the entire Gavronese military from seizing power?"

Six matter-of-fact stares met hers calmly. Tom replied evenly, "That's the mission, ma'am." Then he added, "And I'd appreciate it if you didn't mention anything about it to anyone else, or talk about it outside of this van, in fact. You never know who's listening."

She nodded her understanding, too shell-shocked to verbalize just how crazy she thought they all were. And she'd thought it had been nuts for Jake to single-handedly take out a resurrected drug lord. "So, do you guys have a plan, or are you going to just bomb around in your superhero capes and save the day?"

Tex drawled in a thick twang, "You were right, Howdy. She does have a mouth on her. It's kinda cute. Goes with those big, sweet calf eyes of hers."

She scowled at the lean cowboy type, but couldn't stay annoyed in the face of his laconic grin. "A word of advice, Tex. Don't compare women to cows. Ever." She paused for effect, then added, "You don't do too well with the ladies, do you?"

The other men guffawed as his grin widened. "My wife taught me a long time ago not to mess with a mouthy woman, ma'am."

Jake murmured, "He's married to Congresswoman Kim Stanton of Virginia."

Shannon blinked fast. She'd heard of Kimberly Stanton. The woman was supposed to be a real up-and-comer in Washington. She assessed Tex anew. The dim-witted cowpoke act must be just that—an act. In fact, now that she thought about it, they all looked at her with intelligent, observant eyes. Maybe too observant, as the men's gazes shifted back and forth between her and Jake.

"Here we are," Jake muttered.

Her gaze snapped forward to take in an overgrown driveway onto which they were turning. They were in a quiet neighborhood populated by modest but neat homes that had mostly seen better days. Not the kind of place in which she'd go looking for a team of American commandos, she supposed.

The van stopped in front of a small house surrounded by a heavy screen of trees. It was dark. Deserted looking. The men unloaded quickly, and Tom used a key to let them in the front door. The place smelled musty and was stuffy inside. Nobody turned on any lights until every shade had been pulled and what curtains there were had been closed. The place was furnished, albeit sparsely.

While the other men methodically searched the house from top to bottom—looking for cameras or bugs, she supposed—Mac worked over a window air-conditioning unit, and eventually it coughed to life. Perspiration trickled down Shannon's face as she checked out a filthy bathroom and an equally nasty kitchen. Her first impulse was to scrub both thoroughly, but something in her rebelled at being cast in the status of the little lady who took care of such mundane domestic matters.

But when Doc rolled up his sleeves and fished a sponge and cleaning powder out from under the kitchen sink, she was glad to pitch in. As she attacked the inside of the empty but operable refrigerator, Jake spread out a big map of St. George on the kitchen table, and he and Tom commenced poring over it and talking military strategy. They were trying to figure out how they'd take over the government if they were in charge of the Gavronese army.

It was a strange conversation. And frightening. Within minutes, she had no doubt that if these men had put their minds to it, they could've taken over Gavarone themselves. She actually had to remind herself that these were the good guys.

She and Doc moved on to the lone bathroom, and in short order had it sanitary if not exactly stylish. The thing must've been built in 1950 or so. But the toilet flushed, and Doc assured her that once the water heater had been plugged in for a few hours there'd be hot water in the house. Clearly, the man knew the way to a woman's heart after a long and stressful day—a warm and soothing bath.

When she and Doc emerged from the bathroom, the others were tearing open brown plastic pouches and passing around bags of what looked like dried sawdust. Jake handed one to her. "What's this?" she asked.

"Midnight snack. I think you've got turkey tetrazzini. I've got chili if you'd rather try that."

She frowned down at the plastic bag in her hand.

He added helpfully, "It's freeze-dried. Like backpacking food. You add water and it's actually not that bad. Tons of calories. Or you can try one of these cornflake bars. I find them a little greasy, though."

"Grease and cornflakes? I'll stick with the turkey."

"Good call," he replied wryly.

Was that a hint of humor in his voice? Was the Jake mood pendulum swinging back toward vaguely human? She looked up at him and realized he was standing close to her in something that might almost be interpreted as a protective stance. Bemused, she watched as he poured warm water from a fat teapot into her turkey tetrazzini.

"Now what do I do with it?" she murmured.

"Give it a few minutes to rehydrate, unless you like crunchy turkey," he murmured back low, his voice almost a…caress.

Her toes tingled and a thrill fluttered in her belly. Vivid memory of his hard body against hers and inside hers flashed through her mind. Her breath caught. Only belatedly d manage to mumble, "Thanks for the tip."

She glanced up, and his eyes blazed with white fire for an instant before he turned away sharply and strode out of the kitchen.

Dutch commented quietly, "Don't take offense if he's rude. He's not a very social guy."

"Man, that's an understatement," Mac piped up. "Howdy's the original antisocial type."

"Hell of a shooter though. Best sniper I've ever seen," Tex said.

Tom strolled into the room and added, "He's a good man. Takes his work very seriously."

She looked around at them all. They seemed genuinely fond of Jake, even if they were busy apologizing for him at the moment. "I'd already figured out he's a decent guy. It's just that sometimes he's..."

"Obnoxious?"

"Uncouth?"

"A bastard?"

She laughed. "All of the above."

Tom suggested gently, "Just give him some space. He gets pretty intently focused during a mission. It's nothing personal if he ignores you."

Thing was, he wasn't ignoring her. He was actively being rude to her and pushing her away from him emotionally. She sighed. She wasn't about to air out her relationship issues with Jake to these guys.

Doc added, "Actually, he's pretty intense most of the time."

Last night flashed into her head again. Oh, how true she knew *that* to be!

Jake's disgusted voice floated in from the living room.

up, now. Shannon doesn't need you to
...ne for her. She's doing fine on her own."

...owed on all the men's faces, and five disturbingly
sp... ...gazes turned her way. She stared down fixedly at
her tu... ...mush and prayed she wasn't blushing again.

She was nearing the bottom of her pouch of turkey tetrazzini when Jake returned to the kitchen and approached her reluctantly. "Why don't you go lie down, Shannon? We'll be up most of the night talking through our next moves. It'll be boring military stuff."

His voice was actually kind. Reminiscent of the gentle way he'd acted around her when they first met and she was scared to death of him. A pang of loss speared through her. She wanted this Jake back. She asked wryly, "Has anyone checked the beds to see if they've got fleas?"

Jake shrugged. "This house hasn't been occupied for a while. Fleas drink blood, so without anyone to feed on, the place should be clean."

She winced. She hadn't meant the question literally. But she supposed it was good to know that she wouldn't be flea bitten by morning.

Sudden comprehension lit Jake's eyes. "Do you want me to go back with you and make sure it's safe?"

That wasn't even close to why she'd love to have him retire to the bedroom with her, but if it was all she could get, she'd take it. "That would be nice."

He picked up a shotgun that was standing in the corner. "C'mon. I'll clear the room for you."

Shannon glimpsed eyebrows shooting up all around her but she avoided making direct eye contact with any of the other men. Her face on fire, she followed Jake out of the room. The house had two bedrooms, and Jake led her to the one toward the back of the house. He entered the room first and did, indeed, check under the bed and in the closet for intruders.

He even tested the window and then announced, "Not only is this thing locked, but it feels painted shut. Only way anyone's coming in through here is to break the glass."

She moved over to the bed, surprised to see that someone had made it. The blanket was ratty, but the sheets looked clean. "Doc must have done this," she murmured.

"Actually, I made it for you."

"A sniper who can make beds?" she said lightly. "Who knew you were a man of so many talents?"

Jake ducked his head and looked away. "Get into bed."

She did as he ordered. The mattress sagged toward the middle and the pillow smelled musty, but it was better than sleeping on the floor, she supposed. She jumped, though, when Jake sat down on the edge of the bed and tugged the covers up to her chin.

"What are you doing?" she asked softly.

"Tucking you in."

"Do I get a good-night kiss?"

His gaze jerked to hers. Denial gleamed sharply in his eyes.

"What did I do wrong, Jake? Why are you treating me like this?"

He huffed in what sounded like frustration. "It's not you, Shannon. It's me. I can't—" he continued in a rush "—I don't do relationships. I told you that before."

"That's ridiculous. You do relationships just fine, and there's no reason you shouldn't have one if you want…oh!" She paused as the truth hit her, a knife to the gut. "You don't want a relationship with me. I…oh…I understand. I'm…sorry. I…won't push you anymore."

He shoved a hand through his hair. "No, that's not it. You're fine. Better than fine. Hell, perfect. I just don't…allow myself to have relationships."

He thought she was perfect? Joy and relief exploded inside her, followed closely by confusion. "Why on earth not?"

"They interfere with my job."

"I have to say, Jake, I think you take your job too seriously."

His gaze snapped to hers, shocked. "I *kill* people! That's about as serious a job as a person can have. It's not possible to take my work too seriously!"

"But it is possible to get too immersed in it. To fail to step away from your work and take time to have a personal life."

He snorted.

She tried again. "There are millions of soldiers around the world whose jobs involve killing people, and they have friends. Families. Personal lives."

"Very few of them do what I do. We'll have to agree to disagree on the point."

Maybe he was right. Because she simply did not see his point of view on the matter. Yes, it was grim work. Yes, it was serious, and he ought to take it seriously. But no, he shouldn't let it completely control his life. Heck, ruin his life. She murmured, "I just don't understand why you feel this deep-seated need to punish yourself."

"I don't—" He broke off. "Aww, hell."

He leaned down fast and kissed her. His mouth was hard and unyielding, but as she gave way before the force of it, his lips softened against hers. His tongue slipped between her lips, dancing sweetly across her teeth, caressing her tongue and wringing a soft moan from the back of her throat. His hand plunged into her hair, dragging her up to him. She struggled to free her arms from the blanket, to wrap them around his neck and pull him down to her. But before she could get clear of the tangled sheets, he let her go. Stood up. Stared down at her bleakly.

"It's not you, Shannon. It's me. I can't do this."

He turned around and strode out of the room.

Chapter 15

Jake stumbled out of the bedroom, beating a fast retreat before she could suck him back into that place they'd gone last night where nothing else mattered but the way she felt and the way she made him feel.

That was the crux of the problem. He didn't want to feel anything. He dared not open that Pandora's box. There was too damned much else in his life he was stone-cold terrified of having feelings about.

Tom glanced up when he stalked into the living room. The men had dragged the kitchen table in here so they'd have more room to study the maps spread out across it.

"Everything okay?" his boss asked quietly.

Tom Folly knew him too well for Jake to lie to him. "No. But I've got it under control."

Tom's gaze flickered toward the bedroom then back to him. "If you want to talk, I'm available."

Jake didn't quite manage to restrain a scowl. "If I need a shrink, I'll let you know."

Tom replied soberly, "You do that."

He was not going crazy! This was exactly why he never got involved with women. They were a giant distraction. Made guys act dumber than dirt. Made their teammates think they'd lost their minds.

"Take the first sleep rotation, Howdy," Tom ordered. "You've been working for a while, and the rest of us are just coming on board."

His nerves were jangling, and he emphatically didn't feel like sleeping, but Tom was right. Cursing under his breath, he headed for the front bedroom. Vividly aware of the woman all warm and soft and sexy in her bed on the other side of the wall, he lay down. The mattress was hard and lumpy and cold and didn't do a damned thing to help him relax.

An image of Shannon's sweet face, asleep on his shoulder, rolled through his mind. The image changed, and her face was flushed with passion, her eyes wide with awe as she gazed up at him in the throes of her pleasure.

Stop that! He ripped the image out of his mind, instead picturing Eduardo Ferrare. *Must focus on work.*

He sighed and tried a self-hypnosis routine to put himself to sleep. Then he counted down slowly from a hundred to one in his head in an effort to bore himself to sleep. Then he went with the tried-and-true counting-sheep method. And then he swore at Shannon and at himself for a while. Eventually, he just gave up and allowed her to fill his thoughts. The feel of her skin, the way her body molded to his, the floral scent of her hair, the mind-boggling pleasure he found in her arms. The intoxicating need for more and yet more of her. The utterly foreign and strangely thrilling idea of making this woman his forever. The possessive surge of joy deep in his soul at the thought.

Dammit, he was losing the fight to her. How could one tiny, soft female completely overwhelm him like this? What was it about her that messed him up so bad? Whatever the hold she had over him, he had to figure out its source fast and cut it off at the pass, or he was in big trouble.

He jolted awake some time later. Someone had just tapped the bottom of his foot. His body went to full combat alert instantly. It was Doc.

"Time to brief up," Doc murmured.

"There's a change?"

"Yeah. President of the United States just got a call from President Alviedo asking for help. Alviedo got a tip that the Gavronese military is going to move against him in the morning."

Jake blinked. "What time is it?"

"Four o'clock in the morning, local time."

"What are our orders?"

"We're going to head over to the presidential palace and provide security for Alviedo."

Jake finished tying his boots and stood up. "We're supposed to stop him from being seized?"

"He wants us to stop the entire takeover."

Jake swore. That was a tall order, even for Charlie Squad. "How?"

The two men walked out into the living room. Tom stood before the maps of St. George, which now had a series of red lines inked across them. Without preamble, Jake's boss started talking. "President Alviedo has asked the United States for help, and we've agreed to give it to him. H.O.T. Watch reports increased troop activity at these three Gavronese military installations in the past hour. They conclude that it is the final staging preparations for a military invasion of the city." He traced three thick red lines that converged on the Gavronese parliament building.

"This is the projected path of approach the forces will take."

Tom ran through the expected troop strengths and weaponry they would bring to the job. Then he jabbed a finger at a building circled in red nearly a mile away from the parliament building. "This is the presidential palace. Problem—we don't have enough manpower or firepower to cover both the palace and the parliament building."

Jake frowned. "We need to combine the two into one."

Tom nodded. "Exactly. The plan is to go to the palace, collect Alviedo, and take him over to the parliament building. It's a much bigger building, made of stone, and will withstand an artillery barrage much better than his palace, anyway. Here's a floor plan."

"When do we leave?" Jake asked, already assessing the safest place in the sprawling parliament house to stash the president.

"Ten minutes."

Jake nodded. Good thing he'd cleaned and oiled all his weapons earlier.

"Uhh, what about Shannon?" Doc asked.

Jake answered without hesitation, "We leave her here."

"No, we don't!" a female voice exclaimed from the doorway.

Jake cursed. She must've heard them talking and woken up. Her hair was mussed and she squinted against the room's light, but she looked so delicious he could devour her whole here and now. *Get your mind on the job, dammit.*

The other men all looked over at him. Punting dealing with the irrational female to him, were they? Bastards. "Shannon—" he started.

"Don't take that placating tone with me, Jake Harrington. No way am I sticking around here by myself, wondering what's happening to you—" she corrected hastily "—to all of you. Lucifer Jones is out there somewhere, and I'd go crazy if I had to be alone."

Jake retorted, "We're going to be in the middle of a *war zone*. Tanks and guns will be firing at us. An entire army. You'll be in a thousand times more danger with us than you will be here."

Her eyes were big and dark and irresistible, gleaming with fear. "But you promised, Jake. You said you wouldn't leave me alone."

He closed his eyes against the sight of her. It was entirely unfair of her to bring up that promise now. Chagrin roiled, dangerously close to overwhelming him. He reached deep for control. Calm. He could handle this. "Shannon. You can't come with us."

She marched forward, planted her hands on her hips and glared up at him. "Jake. You can't stop me from coming with you."

In disbelief, he blurted, "You can't possibly force us to take you along."

"I'll go to the neighbor's house and call the press. Warn them that a coup's about to happen and American troops have been deployed to stop it."

Sharp breaths were drawn all around him. Tom said ominously, "We'll tie you to the bed and stuff a gag in your mouth."

Shannon's eyes widened in horror. Goddamn it. Tom didn't have any idea what he'd just said. She lurched forward, racing straight into Jake's arms, and there was no way he could deny her the comfort she sought. Even he wasn't that unfeeling a monster.

He glared at his boss over her head as she shuddered against him.

"What?" Tom asked, confused.

Jake bit out, "She was sexually assaulted in her home a

while back. Tied to her bed for several days. And she thinks the assailant may be in St. George looking for her."

Tom swore freely for several seconds. "Jeez, Shannon. I'm sorry. I didn't know."

She mumbled something against his chest, but Jake couldn't make it out. He did feel his shirt getting damp, however, and she was shaking like a leaf. The strangest sensation came over him. It took him a moment to identify it, in fact. He was definitely feeling sympathy toward her. Empathy. Her silent sobs tore through him like he was tissue being shredded. An errant desire to bury his fist in Tom's mouth actually came over him.

What the hell had she done to him? He was Mr. Cool-Detachment. He'd watched the depths of human suffering and depravity through his sniper's scope over the past two decades and always…*always*…had been able to stand apart from it. Had never let it get to him. His breathing accelerated and his pulse pounded entirely out of control. Was this—no. Couldn't be. Panic? He wasn't afraid of an itty-bitty little thing like her.

But he damned well was afraid of what she did to him. Of what she made him feel. Hell, he was scared stiff of the fact that he was feeling anything at all!

Shannon clung to him so tightly he was actually having a little trouble breathing. Yeah, that was the reason he couldn't seem to draw a full breath.

"Please, Jake," she whispered. "Don't leave me."

His panic deepened. Surely she was only talking about tonight. Not the bigger picture. That was not a plea to stay with her forever, to explore this thing between them and let it grow, let it take him over, let it swallow him whole…. Holy smokes, he was starting to hyperventilate. Get a grip, man!

He forcibly regulated his breathing, slowing his pulse and inhalations as he did in the last moments before he took a shot.

It was a close thing, but he managed to assert his will over his body. Apparently, he'd waited too long to answer, though, for her body tensed and her shaking intensified along with her jerky sobs.

"Please, Jake. I'm begging you. I'd rather get shot and die fast at your side than stay here and die by slow degrees."

"It won't be that bad to stay behind," he argued.

"Yes, it will. How am I supposed to wait and wonder, knowing you're in harm's way? Knowing that an entire army is coming after you?"

Her words were simultaneously acid and balm to his soul. He emphatically didn't want to put her in the very harm's way she spoke of. Every cell in his being screamed at him to keep her far, far away from danger. But at the same time, he was amazed, humbled even, that she would worry about him so much. What had he ever done to deserve the care and concern of a woman like her? He didn't deserve her love any more than he deserved to have a life of his own.

Her arms tightened around him convulsively, and he was reminded of their incredible night together, of how she had wrapped her entire body around his, binding him to her so intimately that their very souls had merged into one.

His need to protect her, to be with her, to never let her go, surged to the fore, completely swamping all of his objections to her coming along with Charlie Squad. "All right." He sighed. "You can come with us."

His teammates stared at him as if he'd just grown a third eye in the middle of his forehead. Grins started to spread. Mac was the first to speak. "Holy crap. She has breached the mighty Fort Harrington. Congratulations, Shannon! Never thought I'd live to see it."

Someone thumped him on the back.

The others joined in with various jocular comments that set his teeth on edge and brought thoughts of violence against his teammates to mind. A comment floated past about it being a sure sign of true love when a guy couldn't bear to be parted from his girl.

His head whipped around at that. He snapped, "Have any of you got a better idea than taking her with us?"

None of the other men would make eye contact with him. And it wasn't as if any of them could say a hell of a lot about taking a woman with them into the line of fire. They'd all done it at one time or another themselves.

Contrarily, their joking about it made him all the more determined to take her with him on this mission. No doubt about it, this was sheer insanity. He peeled Shannon away from his chest far enough to look down at her. "But there have to be a few ground rules. You'll do exactly what I say the moment I tell you to do it. No questions, no hesitation. You stick with me at all times, and you do your best to stay out of my way. No hysteria. No falling apart when things get bad. Got it?"

She nodded gamely.

The panic he was holding at bay by a thin thread threatened to overtake him again. Crap. He was in no condition to go into combat, let alone kill anyone. "And bring the pistol I gave you."

Good God, this was a giant mistake. But what else was he supposed to do?

Chapter 16

Seated in the front of the van again, Shannon glanced back at the heavily armed commandos Jake's buddies had morphed into over the past few minutes. They were grim, silent and intensely focused on the job ahead.

Jake was driving. Frankly, she'd been shocked when he'd relented and agreed to let her come with them. Not that she was complaining. She'd meant it when she'd said she'd rather die by his side in a blaze of glory than stay alone in that house and die by inches. Although she had to admit she was scared silly of what she was getting herself into.

"The palace is in sight," Jake announced.

Tom moved forward between the seats. He used a pair of binoculars to look all around as they approached the presidential palace. "We're clear. Alviedo said he'd have some of his trusted personal guards meet us at the delivery entrance."

Jake nodded. "That's around the corner."

The van made the turn, and Tom held up his left hand. He made some sort of signal with it, and Shannon started as weapons clicked en masse. She glanced over questioningly at Jake, who murmured, "Those were the safeties coming off our weapons. You might want to go in the back and lie down now."

She did as he suggested, switching places with Tom, although it was awkward with the bulky Kevlar vest swathing her. She and Jake had argued sharply about her taking his vest, but he'd been adamant. She'd caught the stunned looks his teammates had thrown their way when he'd snapped that he was taking care of her and that was all there was to it, but no one had said anything about it. Still, she felt guilty leaving him unprotected like this. He'd insisted that anyone out to kill him wouldn't hit his vest but would blow his head off. As if that was supposed to comfort her.

Tom reported tersely, "Four men at the guard shack carrying semiautomatic rifles."

Nobody moved, but the tension level rose around her noticeably. Jake rolled down his window and exchanged quiet words with someone outside. Then the van was rolling again.

"We're in," Tom announced.

The men around her breathed a sigh of relief. Her sigh was at least as fervent as theirs. The back door of the van opened.

"President Alviedo?" Doc asked.

"You are the men of Charlie Squad, no?" a resonant voice responded from the darkness outside.

"That's correct," Doc answered in flawless Spanish.

"On behalf of my country, I thank you for your assistance," the politician answered.

"Get in," Tom ordered briskly.

"My men. They will come with me?"

"No, sir. We'll take over your personal security from here. Your men need to coordinate with the forces within your military that are loyal to you and gather those troops. I'd suggest they rally at the entrance to the parliament building as soon as possible. If they have time, they should prepare several fallback positions within the building, should the fire from outside become too intense."

Shannon saw all three of the guards nod their understanding.

The president of Gavarone crawled into the van beside her on hands and knees. "Who have we here? A woman?" he exclaimed. "Is she one of the American female commandos I have heard whispers of?"

She smiled lamely and replied in Spanish, "Sorry. I'm just a civilian who was in the wrong place at the wrong time. My name's Shannon McMahon."

"It is a pleasure to meet you, Miss McMahon."

"Likewise, sir." She couldn't believe she was trading pleasantries with the president of a country on the floor of an unmarked van.

Tom spoke from up front. "We'll be at the parliament building in five minutes. We're going to take you in the private entrance around back. How far is it to your office from there?"

"Up three flights of stairs and then through to the west side of the building. Won't it be dangerous for me to stay there? My office has large windows and faces the front of the building."

Tom grinned. "Trust me. We won't be keeping you there. But we thought it might be a good idea for you to tape some sort of statement from your office to be released on national television in case your country is in need of reassurance later today."

Alviedo grinned and winked at her. "So. The commandos are adept politicians, as well."

Tom shrugged. "Our training includes psychological operations and methods for swaying large crowds."

Jake added dryly, "It's amazing the calming effect a good barrage of heavy-weapons fire can have on an angry mob. Makes them rethink their politics every time."

"Let us hope it does not come to that," the president replied grimly.

"If Eduardo Ferrare is behind this coup," Jake replied, "you can be certain it will. The man will stop at nothing to get what he wants."

Alviedo commented, "Your president said he is alive, but I cannot believe it."

Jake glanced over his shoulder. "Believe it. I've seen the man with my own eyes. Here in St. George. Alive and kicking as recently as a day ago."

"How—" the president started to ask, but Tom waved him to silence, saying, "We're here, sir. Shannon, I need you to stick to President Alviedo like glue. Charlie Squad will form a cordon around both of you. We're going to hustle you inside, so be prepared to move quickly."

"Okay," she answered. The reality of what she'd gotten herself into was starting to sink in as Jake's teammates jumped out of the van in the pre-dawn darkness and took up defensive positions, their rifles at the ready.

She and Alviedo clambered out of the van, and indeed, they all but ran into the building. Jake had his hand on the top of her head the whole time, shoving her down into an awkward half crouch that made the maneuver even scarier.

They gained the safety of the building's interior, and Jake let her stand upright. "You okay?" he murmured.

She nodded that she was. And then they were on the move again, racing down a darkened hall to a bank of elevators. The president produced a plastic key card, and one of the doors opened for him. Mac stayed outside the elevator.

Tom said, "You'll disable these and then join us?"

Mac replied, already prying the cover off one of the sets of controls, "This will take five minutes."

"I'll send a team down for you if you're not in the president's office in ten," Tom retorted.

The elevator doors slid closed, and the group rode to the third floor in silence. Jake was first out of the elevator, crouching low and spinning to his right. Tex followed, spinning left. It looked like something out of a Hollywood movie and felt as surreal. Tom gestured her and the president forward. They moved fast down an ornately decorated hall to the president's offices. Alviedo's key card let them in here, as well.

"Will you disable these locks, too?" the man asked.

Tom shook his head. "We'll leave here as soon as you've taped your message. Then we'll take out the locks to make it look like you're holed up inside."

"Does one of you know how to operate a television camera?" Alviedo asked.

Doc grinned. "That would be me."

Tom added smoothly, "My headquarters took the liberty of drafting several short statements for you. Of course, you should look them over and feel free to make any additions or changes you'd like."

Alviedo looked surprised. "You men are thorough, aren't you?"

Tom answered for all of them. "We try, sir."

Shannon was relegated to a chair in the corner for the next half hour while President Alviedo taped three statements. One explained that a coup was under way and asked all citizens to stay inside for their safety. A second one explained that other governments had condemned the attempted takeover and were providing support for the legitimate government. The address also named Eduardo Ferrare and several of his henchmen as the financiers and driving force behind this attack on the government.

The third and final statement by Alviedo declared that the coup had been defeated and that his loyal forces were firmly in control. She sincerely hoped they got to broadcast that statement before the day was over. The tapes were played back, declared acceptable by Alviedo, and then burned onto multiple DVD disks. Jake had slipped out not long after the taping started and didn't return until they were just finishing up.

"Got them?" Tom murmured.

Jake nodded back.

"You know what to do," Tom responded.

She really wished these guys wouldn't talk in riddles like that. But on the other hand, maybe ignorance was bliss. She wasn't at all sure she wanted to know what they had planned by way of stopping an army. The group stepped back out into the main hallway.

"Come with me, Shannon," Jake ordered.

She looked at him in surprise. "We're not going with the others?"

"Nope."

He took off down the hall toward the very front of the building, and she tagged along. Soon the others disappeared in the opposite direction. "Where are we going?" she asked.

"Up."

"Up where?"

"You'll see."

She sighed. The taciturn sniper was back. Although for once maybe that wasn't a bad thing. She followed him up several flights of stairs. They emerged on the top floor of the building and moved quickly to a window looking down on Parliament Square.

"What are we doing here?"

"Setting up shop."

"Could you please speak in plain English?"

He glanced over at her humorously. "Welcome to my world, darlin'."

He knelt down and opened up a long case. Inside lay a gun, a really big one, in three pieces. He commenced screwing the pieces together, and in a few seconds had a weapon that was easily six feet long set up on a low tripod and pointed down at the street below.

Without glancing up, he asked, "Do you have the pistol I gave you?"

She patted the holster under her left armpit. "Right here."

"Don't be shy about using that if you need to. Fire it in self-defense and only at close range. You won't hit anything else without training. Do you remember what I showed you about taking the safety off?"

She nodded.

"Do it now."

Fumbling at the leather snap, she loosed the pistol, pulled out its frightening weight and pushed the safety to its firing position. She holstered the weapon once more but left the snap off.

"Now for the hide," he murmured.

She watched as he laid out a beige net woven through with strips of matching cloth. It was close in color to the roof stones making up the window sill and about eighty square feet. He held up one edge of it. "In you go."

She frowned up at him.

"Do you want to stay exposed and get picked off by the first person with a gun who spots you looking out the window?"

She dropped to her knees and crawled under the net. Thankfully, Jake joined her after mounting his gun on a tripod and cutting a round hole in the window for the gun barrel. His body was as warm and strong and drugging as she remembered. He didn't seem similarly affected by her, though. He merely placed his right eye to the rubber cup of the telescope-y thing on top of the gun and looked down at the street for a long time.

Eventually, he touched his throat mike. "All clear," he announced quietly.

She released a relieved breath. "Now what?"

"Now we wait. Catch a nap if you want."

"Right. Like I'm going to be able to sleep when I'm smashed against you from head to foot."

Loaded silence greeted that comment.

And then it occurred to her that he was as trapped under this narrow net with her as she was with him. And she wasn't above taking advantage of it. "What gives, Jake?"

"What do you mean?" he asked cautiously.

"Why do you keep blowing hot and cold with me? One minute you act like a human being, and the next you're back to being a block of ice."

He answered stiffly, "I don't know what you're talking about."

She laughed, albeit without much humor. "Sure you do. Don't try to B.S. me. I've been a teacher far too long for that."

He closed his eyes. Rested his forehead against his gun. "I'm supposed to be up here getting ready to take out the leaders of the coup, and you want to talk about our relationship."

Dang it. He was right. Heavy silence fell between them. It stretched out, oppressive and uncomfortable, and she didn't have the faintest idea how to break it.

Finally, he muttered, "If you're not going to sleep, you might as well make yourself useful."

"How?"

He passed her two photographs, both men in Gavronese Army uniforms. "You've already seen what Ferrare looks like. We believe these two generals are the leaders of the coup. If you see any of them, let me know. Call them F, G1 or G2. Those are their code names for today's purposes. Just tell me which one of them you see and where."

Shannon took the pictures and stared at the faces, trying to burn them into her memory as best she could. It filled the void for a little while. But eventually she passed the pictures back to him and they were back to square one. This silence was going to drive her crazy. Desperate for something to talk about, she asked, "How do you prepare to do your job?"

He lurched and threw her a frightening look. The cold killer from the alley was back. She recoiled in dismay. He blinked several times, and the icy stare finally cleared from his eyes.

He spoke woodenly. "I wipe my mind clean of all emotion. No thoughts. I calm myself completely. Slow my pulse and breathing. And then I wait for the shot."

She cast about for another question. "How do you know when to shoot?"

"In most cases, I'm green-lighted well in advance of the moment. Like tonight. I already have permission to take out those men I showed you. I wait until a clean shot presents itself, and then I take it."

"Do you ever hesitate? Pass up a shot? Second-guess yourself?"

He glanced down at her in complete incomprehension. "Of course not."

"So, you never have doubts about anyone you kill?"

"It's not my call. Someone else makes the decision to kill them. I'm just the instrument of their decision."

She pounced on that. "Then why do you take it so personally when you shoot someone?"

"I don't take it personally," he retorted with more heat than she'd have expected.

She held up a finger. "Wait. Wait. Yup, there it goes."

"What are you talking about?" he snapped.

"My B.S. alarm just went off. Of course you take it personally, Jake. Why else would you insist on denying yourself any kind of a life? You're punishing yourself."

"Will you *please* get off of that soapbox?"

"As soon as you climb down off it with me."

He shook his head. "I knew I was going to regret bringing you along."

She sensed she'd pushed him about as far as he was going to stand for, and besides, he was up here to do an important job. And if he needed to clear his mind, this argument wasn't helping. She subsided beside him. Ultimately, she did close her eyes and try to get a little sleep, but it was hopeless.

Dawn was just breaking when Jake murmured beside her, "Here they come."

That yanked her to full consciousness in a millisecond. Perhaps two hundred soldiers were gathering in front of the parliament building, filling up the broad plaza with bristling guns.

She looked down and gasped.

"Don't be alarmed. At least not yet. They're the good guys."

"They look pretty scary."

Jake's mouth twitched. "Wait till the bad guys get here."

"Is there going to be a shootout in the plaza, winner take all?" she asked incredulously.

"Nah. Charlie Squad will let these guys in momentarily.

They'll defend the president from inside the parliament building."

In the next few minutes the plaza emptied as the loyalist troops moved into the building beneath her. Relative silence fell once more. Birds were starting to chirp and delivery trucks were driving past as if this were just another normal morning.

And then a new noise intruded upon the morning. A low-throated rumble like a freight train gathering speed. She looked through the binoculars Jake had given her, spotted the source of the noise and gasped.

A line of army trucks was snaking down the broad boulevard toward them. She counted twenty-one vehicles, and the end of the line continued out of sight around a corner. Her heart leaped into her throat. What on earth had she gotten herself into?

Jake glanced over at her. He must have seen her fear because he sighed and said, "If you want, you can head downstairs and take cover with the rest of the team."

She took a deep breath. "I'll stay with you."

He nodded tersely and then plastered his eye to his gun sight. "Showtime," he muttered. And then he began relaying a steady stream of information to his teammates. "Incoming. I've got visual on a truck convoy… Thirty trucks in sight. No more than twenty troops in each… No tanks yet… Another line coming in from the north. Just rounding the corner of Ascension Avenue… Tanks in this column. Two of them… Affirmative. Just two."

A deep, distant boom reverberated from somewhere behind them. Shannon jumped.

"They're firing on the presidential palace," Jake murmured to her. "They don't know we've got Alviedo over here yet."

Just then a loud noise erupted below, and Shannon cringed against his side.

"That was a little gunfire. No big deal. And, honey, you seriously need to not bump into me like that. I could kill the wrong guy if you do that while I'm taking a shot."

Horror flowed through her. She could be responsible for the murder of an innocent? Ohmigosh. She whispered, "When will you start shooting?"

"When the generals in charge of this circus show themselves."

"When will that be?"

He shrugged.

Using the binoculars, she scanned the mob of soldiers, so much larger than the last one, milling about in the plaza, toting weapons and acting macho. They were so young for the most part. Boys, really. Pawns of power players like Eduardo Ferrare and his general friends.

More and more trucks poured into the plaza in front of parliament and more and more soldiers poured out of them, shouting and waving guns around in the air. It was terrifying to watch them whip themselves up into a frenzy. Somebody shouted a political diatribe through a bullhorn, but she couldn't make out most of what the man said. The mood became uglier below.

Jake murmured into his microphone, "They're acting like they've figured out the president slipped through their fingers.

She was dying to ask him what he expected would happen now but didn't want to disturb him.

"I've got visual on G2," Jake muttered.

She looked off to their right and saw a Jeep coming fast down the boulevard. Jake swung his rifle toward the vehicle, and then his body went utterly still. His concentration was fierce, and she drew away from him another few inches to let him do his thing. And maybe that was why out of the corner of her eye she caught the slight movement off to her left.

"Jake!" she screamed as two men burst through the stairwell doorway pointing guns at them. And they looked pissed.

Chapter 17

A bead of sweat rolled down the side of Jake's face, and it itched. Odd. He had always been able to ignore small annoyances like that. Concentrating fiercely, he put the slow drip out of his mind. He could do this, dammit. He could shut out the world and do his job. Focus. Breathe in. No body. No feeling. No thoughts. Exhale. His body shook with the effort of forcing Shannon out of his consciousness. He swore at himself. He'd just thought about her again. He was losing it here.

Failure was not an option. Discipline, dammit. *Find the strength.* Block out everything. *Everything.* Him and the gun and the target. Nothing else existed in the entire world but the three of them.

A high-pitched noise registered vaguely beside him. Must. Not. Look.

Sweating and shaking, he forced his mind to stay the course. Focus on the target. The general was coming into range now.

Two final breaths: one for his target, one for him. He exhaled slowly. Began the easy pull through the trigger. A caress, really. The delicate touch of Death.

His rifle barely lurched against his cheek. It was a close-range shot, and the general's head vaporized. In its place hung a brief pall of red mist that started to dissipate immediately. Life. No life. Poof. Just like that.

A deafening explosion of noise right beside him jolted him violently out of his trance. What the—?

"Jake!" Shannon screamed.

Disoriented, he reacted more out of reflex than out of conscious thought. He rolled onto his back and reached for his sidearm all in one movement. And took in the sight before him in a moment of horrified comprehension.

Two soldiers had burst into the hallway, both carrying pistols. Shannon had shot one of them—a nice shot to the gut, actually—and that guy was rolling around on the ground, bleeding. The second man had paused for an instant to stare at his buddy but was moving again, almost on them, and starting to dive for Shannon. Jake aimed for the guy's shoulder—a shot that would disarm him and stop him but not kill him. Shannon had already seen too much violence at his hands. The hit caused the guy to drop his weapon but didn't take the guy down. Surprisingly, the guy didn't stop, either.

Jake swore. That hadn't been the plan. He leaped to his feet, jumping across Shannon to get between her and the hostile soldier. The guy dived, slamming into Jake's shins and knocking Jake's pistol out of his hands.

Shannon scrambled out of the way as Jake took a step back from his attacker to assess him. He registered her terrified sobs and something cracked inside him. Something big. Like the wing spar of a jet or the main beam of a ship breaking. The part that supported all the rest of him, the part that gave him spine and direction, his emotional backbone. Busted clean through.

Jake's brain finally caught up with his body and started functioning again. *Holy crap. She'd killed a man for him.* For him. He'd taken a sweet, gentle, innocent woman and turned her into a killer. An unwilling one who abhorred violence. How was she ever supposed to live with that? How was *he* supposed to live with it?

It was the final straw.

He'd finally committed the last, unpardonable sin. He'd corrupted an innocent.

Something solid connected with his jaw. The soldier, surging up from below, had punched him. Hard. Good hit. Jake's head snapped to the side, and the entire left half of his face felt like it had exploded.

He deserved worse than the shadowy half life he allowed himself. He deserved to *die.* The soldier let loose with a body blow and another swing at his face. Jake stepped into the blows. The pain was a fire burning away everything he was. He embraced it. And found peace in its agony.

"Jake! What are you doing?" a voice screamed.

Shannon. He looked over at her. Mumbled, "I'm sorry."

She scrambled to her feet. The pistol wobbled violently in her hands as she pointed at him and his attacker. No. No bullets! That would be too easy an end for him.

"Fight back!" she shouted.

He snorted. The last time he'd fought back in front of her he'd scared her to death. She hated violence. He would never do that to her again. Another punishing blow to his nose broke it, and his eyes watered copiously.

Shannon was on her feet now, begging and crying for him to fight. She didn't understand. This was for her. He'd committed the one, final, unforgivable sin, and now he had to pay. Jake Harrington, army officer, sniper, murderer, had to disappear.

Even the guy before him seemed not to understand. The soldier's battle rage was giving way to confusion over why his opponent wasn't fighting back.

"Hit me," Jake growled.

The soldier hesitated.

"*Hit* me!"

The soldier took a step forward, cocking his fist.

Bang!

The shot came from just behind Jake, and a giant blossom of red erupted in the middle of the guy's chest. The soldier stared at Jake in shock for a moment before his legs collapsed. Then he crumpled to the ground as Jake whirled, furious. "What the hell did you do that for?" he demanded.

Tears streaming down her face, Shannon dropped the pistol and sobbed, "He was killing you."

"But that's what I deserve."

Shannon launched herself at him then, pummeling his chest with her fists. "What's *wrong* with you? Don't you dare die on me!"

He blinked at her, uncomprehending.

"You get back over to the gun and take out the generals in charge of this insanity before hundreds of kids die down there. You hear me?"

A male voice rumbled in his earpiece, "What's going on up there, Howdy? We heard gunfire."

Tom Folly's voice, so familiar, so long a voice of camaraderie and brotherhood, finally penetrated the fugue state wrapping around Jake's mind. "Uhh. Yeah," he mumbled. "Shannon shot two guys, actually. They're wearing army uniforms. Must have had a few pro-coup infiltrators in among the loyalist soldiers who got let into the building."

"Say your status," Tom barked.

His status. Jake laughed aloud. "Who the hell knows?"

"Howdy. What's wrong with you?" Tom bit out. "We have reports that G1 is en route to the plaza. Alviedo and our own intel analysts believe that if we take him out, the coup will collapse. Get to position two. I need you to eliminate him."

Twenty years of conditioning took over. *At all costs, he must follow orders.* Jake moved, robotlike, toward his sniper rig, breaking it down mechanically.

"What are you doing?" she gasped in horror.

"Moving to the roof. Can't shoot from the same spot twice. Their snipers will be looking for me here." He gazed up at her, his eyes a vast, empty desert. "Get out of here. I've hurt you enough. Go downstairs. Leave the building. Run from this place. Run from me."

She stared at him in open agony, but he gave no ground. He would not harm her anymore. No more violence, no more blood in her world on his account. He looked on as, slowly, her hope died, draining out of her face and then her entire body. She turned, her feet shuffling and her shoulders slumped like an old woman's, and left.

A single thought formed in his brain.

When this was over, he was going to find himself a suicide mission to volunteer for.

Shannon didn't know what to do. Something was terribly wrong with Jake. He'd been prepared to let that soldier kill him. He'd been almost catatonic, barely able to function. And somehow it was all her fault. He was going to fail his mission and all those hundreds of boy soldiers below were going to slaughter each other because of it. He was right. She had to leave him alone. Let him do his job. Let him be what and who he was.

She'd been a fool to think she could draw out the warm, loving man within him. It had been a terrible mistake to try, and apparently she'd nearly destroyed him in the process. How could she have been so stupid?

She stumbled down the staircase all the way to the ground floor, emerging just inside the main entrance of the parliament building. A television news crew jolted when she opened the stairwell door beside them and she startled at their unexpected presence.

"What are you doing here?" she and a reporter demanded of each other simultaneously.

The reporter spoke first. "We're leaving the building now. We've been given a white flag by each side to pass outside unharmed and carry the president's taped message to the generals out there." The man jerked his head toward the front door. "You want to come with us? Stay here and you'll be shot to pieces. The military's got tanks rolling this way and they're going to blow the building to smithereens."

And Jake was somewhere inside. A sob escaped her before she could plaster her hand across her mouth. She had no idea where in the building the rest of Charlie Squad was holed up or she'd join them. Worse, she was on the verge of throwing up at the memory of shooting those men. As much as every cell of her being screamed at her to stay near Jake, she had to get away from here.

She nodded her acceptance of the reporter's offer and fell in beside his cameraman. "How in the hell did you get in here?" the guy asked her as they emerged onto the front steps.

A thousand rifles came to bear on them as they stepped into the bright morning sun with a deafening chorus of metallic snicks. A man standing behind a Jeep raised both hands and shouted in Spanish for the troops to hold their fire.

Shannon looked over at him. G1. The general in charge of this whole circus. She resisted glancing up at the roof lest she give away Jake's position. Where the general was standing now, no one on the roof would have a line of fire on him. The general needed to move so Jake could take him out.

Inspiration struck, and she murmured to the reporter, "Hey, there's the head honcho over behind that Jeep. Maybe you can get a quick interview with him. What a scoop that would be!"

The reporter's gaze narrowed speculatively. "C'mon, Ramon," he said to the cameraman. "Let's go get us a Pulitzer."

She tagged along, doing her darnedest to look like she belonged with the pair of men. Hopefully nobody would notice that a team of two journalists had turned into a party of three.

The general's position was toward the back of the plaza. Civilians were crowding the streets leading to the square. Whether they were merely curious onlookers or supporters of the coup hoping to get their piece of the action, she couldn't tell. An awful lot of them were holding up video cameras and cell phones like they were mainly interested in collecting YouTube footage. They seemed unaware of the carnage that could be imminent.

The cameraman panned his lens across the crowd and got an immediate reaction. The crowd roared and surged forward, shoving past the soldiers trying to hold them back. People poured into the square, filling up what little space remained and causing a crush that jostled Shannon from all sides. She lost sight of the general in the chaos.

Standing on her tiptoes, she tried frantically to spot G1. To see if there was anything she could do to draw him out, to give Jake the clear shot he needed on the guy. Although how Jake was going to find and kill a single person in this writhing mob, she had no idea. Still. If she could help him in any way, she was determined to do it.

Over there. She thought she spied the broad nose and deep-set eyes of the general. She pushed through the crowd, which was more civilian than military on this side of the plaza. It was worse than Times Square on New Year's Eve and just as boisterous. Buffeted this way and that, she pushed as hard as she could to force her way forward.

It took her a moment to realize it when an arm wrapped around her waist from behind.

"Well, well, well," a deep voice drawled in her ear. "Look who we've got here."

Horror worse than what she'd felt when she killed a man exploded inside her. She knew that voice. *Lucifer.*

Jake cradled his gun, going through the motions of searching for target G1, but half-dead inside. Sweet Shannon. He hoped she'd get over the horror of what he'd made her do, someday. She'd gotten over what Lucifer Jones had done to her…

…except what he'd done to her had been so much worse than what Jones had done. Lucifer had hurt her body. *He had hurt her mind.* He'd forced her to confront and embrace the violence of his world against her will without ever giving her a choice.

Never again, Shannon. I promise you, my love.

He paused. Love? Who'd have guessed he'd ever fall in love? And with a woman so tremendously different from him? It wasn't an experience he'd expected to have in his lifetime.

It had hurt worse than anything he'd ever experienced to watch her disappear down that stairwell. It had ripped his heart out. But there was peace in knowing that he'd stood his ground and done the right thing, no matter how much it hurt him. He'd stayed the course. He registered satisfaction in a distant, detached sort of way.

Methodically, he scanned the crowd face by face, concentrating on clusters of activity that seemed to be centering around various important individuals. He figured G1 would either be right up front on the steps of the parliament building or way at the back of the plaza. He finished scanning the front ranks of the soldiers and shifted his attention to the back of the crowd. It was easy to pick out the lone news crew in the plaza, and predictably, the activity was heavy around them as civilians and soldiers alike tried to get their fifteen seconds of fame.

There. Was that a glimpse of G1? He zeroed in on the particularly turbulent section of the crowd. A determined phalanx of civilians was shoving forward toward the spot where he thought he might have seen the general. If G1 was in that area, he'd ducked behind cover again. Must've taken a lesson from G2's death a few minutes ago.

Frankly, Jake was surprised that the Gavronese military's own snipers weren't hard at work picking him off yet. Apparently, the rebel generals hadn't anticipated his sort of resistance to their little takeover.

Yup. That was definitely G1 behind that Jeep.

He swept the area immediately behind the vehicle, and lurched. He knew that face. And that one. And that one. Eduardo Ferrare's personal bodyguards. Had the man himself come down to the plaza to watch the show? Stunned, Jake scanned the crowd.

Ferrare. At the sight of his nemesis, fury stabbed Jake, piercing the fog that enveloped his brain. Before he went off and threw himself into a blaze of glory, he was taking that bastard down. The two of them could go to hell together. A fitting end for both of them. Too bad he couldn't take Lucifer Jones down before he checked out, too.

Ferrare shifted, momentarily disappearing behind one of his bodyguards, the largest one, a towering hulk of a man who, from this angle, reminded him of…

Sonofa— That was Lucifer's brother. Fiercely, Jake scanned the man's immediate vicinity until he found what he was looking for. *Who* he was looking for. The bastard was a few years older than the pictures H.O.T. Watch had sent him, his hair a little longer than the prison photos, but it couldn't be anyone else. Jake's jaw tightened. Two more shots, then. One for Ferrare and one for Jones.

But first the mission. G1. There he was, just to Ferrare's right. Jake started to swing his gun away from Lucifer, but his attention was captured as Lucifer suddenly bent over, moving jerkily. It looked like something had knocked him off balance. The mob shifted slightly, and red haze erupted behind Jake's eyelids. Lucifer had Shannon wrapped in his arms!

"The tanks are here," Tex's voice announced tersely over his earpiece. "The killing field's about to go live."

And thousands of soldiers and civilians were going to get caught in the crossfire. Including Shannon.

Tom bit out, "It's up to you, Howdy. If you've got any kind of a bead on G1, take the shot *now*."

Jesus. Shannon or a civil war? Love or duty? One shot. One solution. Torn in two, he wrestled furiously with his choice. Finally, barely able to see through the tears streaming down his cheeks, he took quick aim. And fired.

Chapter 18

Terror exploded inside Shannon. Her entire body shook, and she couldn't draw breath to do anything other than think *ohmigod, ohmigod, ohmigod...*

He was stronger than she remembered. Bigger. Even scarier. And she'd spent seven years having nightmares over him. He was going to drag her away from here. Away from Jake, who'd promised to protect her. Away from the new life she'd made for herself. And he was going to kill her. There wasn't the slightest doubt in her mind that he would finish what he'd started all those years ago—torturing her to death.

Anger at Jake for breaking his word, for not being there for her when this monster showed up again, flashed through her mind. And then anger at herself came. She'd thought she was so smart fleeing to a war-torn South American country to hide from Jones. She'd been so sure he'd never find her. But she hadn't counted on his persistence, nor the Jones brothers' criminal connections. Stupid, stupid, stupid.

And now she was going to die.

At just about any time in the past seven years, she'd have surrendered to that idea fairly readily. She'd lived in hell, trapped in the tiny, silent box her life had become. Many times she'd considered ending it all herself. But that was before Jake. Before he'd woken her from her long emotional slumber, before he'd torn back the haze obscuring her life and showed her all the vibrant joy and pain and *living* she was missing. In trying to get him to live again, she'd learned to live herself.

But she'd failed him. He'd slipped into the black night of his soul, a place from which she had no idea how to retrieve him. Defeat washed over her as Lucifer laughed bitterly behind her and started to drag her backward toward the edge of the plaza.

She'd come out here with a vague idea of helping Jake get a clean shot at his target—which was a ridiculous idea, she supposed. But such was love. People did ridiculous things in the name of it. Apparently, they died in the name of it, too. Lord knew, the greater part of her had died when Jake ordered her away from him.

"You thought you could get away from me?" Lucifer snarled in her ear.

Whatever. Compared to losing Jake, this man was the least of her concerns. "You don't scare me, Lucifer," she answered tiredly. "Just do your worst and get it over with. I'm done running from you. Let's end this."

The arms around her slackened in surprise. "You think you ain't gonna be fun if you don't fight? You're wrong. I'll have my fun anyway. Never did forget how sweet you screamed for me."

An involuntary shudder rippled down her spine.

"Never had another woman who screamed like you.

Maybe I'll find me one down here in this hellhole when I'm done with you."

The thought of him doing to another woman all the horrific things he'd done to her infuriated Shannon. It was bad enough that she'd had to go through it, but no other woman should have to endure it. It was practically her civic duty to kill this monster before he tortured and killed anyone else. Comprehension broke across her brain.

This was why Jake killed. Not to exorcise his own demons. To save other people from having to carry the same demons in their souls that he did.

He thought he was a monster. But he was wrong. He was a saint. He was sacrificing his soul to save everyone else's. If only she could make him see that. There had to be a way to get through to him.

But not if Lucifer killed her today. Not if she died. Who would save Jake then?

Abrupt memory of Jake laughing at her paltry self-defense training burst across her mind. *You civilians. You don't understand what it means to fight to the death. You're not willing to take the collateral damage—the pain—to win. That's why people like me always defeat people like you.*

Well, she wasn't dying today, thank you very much. She had a hero to save from himself.

Shannon exploded into motion, kicking and flailing, her heels and elbows connecting painfully with hard ribs and shins. Lucifer grunted and tightened his hold on her. "Scream all you want. Nobody's gonna hear you in this crowd."

She didn't waste the breath it would take to scream. She was going down fighting. Right here. Right now. She jerked her right arm free and threw a fist up and back as hard as she could. It felt like her knuckle broke, but so did Lucifer's nose.

"I'll break you in half," he howled in rage.

She figured since he hadn't already done it, she might just be a little harder to break than he'd expected. Something huge and hard slammed into the side of her head, his fist probably, and she saw stars. Her right ear felt like it had exploded. She fought on grimly.

"I hope you've got a hell of a good reason to live, Lucifer," she ground out, "because I know I've got one. You're going to have to kill me to stop me."

A gunshot echoed across the plaza just then, followed immediately by screams and groans. A shout went up that another generalissimo had been shot. Shouts for doctors and ambulances accompanied that, and some of the fervor seemed to go out of the mob. In a detached corner of her mind, Shannon registered that doctors and medics would be hopeless. Jake was very, very good at what he did. If Jake had taken the shot, the general was dead.

Another shot rang out, and the resulting commotion was much closer. Men shouted crazily all around her. The crowd shoved frantically, and she gathered that someone else had been shot very close by. Whoever it was, it had thrown the cluster of big, grim men in her vicinity into chaos.

Lucifer's arms loosened without warning, and he flung her to the ground. Startled, she rolled away from the vicious kick she knew was coming and fetched up hard against a wall of shins. The crowd was starting to panic, and she was in real danger of being trampled. The side of her face was on fire; she must've scraped it on the pavement. Ignoring pain that under normal circumstances would have taken her breath away, she popped up to her feet.

"You think you can take me with your housewife tae kwon do?" Lucifer laughed.

"No. I know I can take you with my will to live and superior intelligence."

That took him aback. Enough to pause and stare at her momentarily. The crowd surged at her back, shoving her forward practically into Lucifer's chest. He grinned, and his humongous fists came up to break her face. She dodged, going low. She was so much smaller than him, maybe she could turn that into an advantage. She charged forward, ramming her fist—with the entire weight of her body behind it—into his genitals as hard as she could.

Lucifer screamed and doubled over, swearing.

Stunned, Shannon staggered back. Wait, she wasn't supposed to stop. That was more of that not-committed-to-the-kill civilian behavior. She joined her fists together and brought both hands down on the back of Lucifer's neck as hard as she could. She envisioned knocking his head off his neck as she took the swing. The big man dropped like a stone at her feet. She almost stopped again but told herself to keep fighting.

She stomped on his neck with her right foot. Revulsion bubbled in her gut, but grimly she fought on, pummeling him every way she knew how. She invented a few new moves while she was at it. The guy was so big and so thick she feared she wasn't really damaging him. That he would wake up and get back to his feet so mad he truly would break her in half.

When her will to continue the beating flagged, Shannon dredged up her old memories of all the horrors he'd inflicted on her and used that to fuel her tired limbs. She refused to give up.

Jake slammed a ninety-two-grain sniper round into his weapon and chambered it all in one movement. He plastered his eyes to his sight and swung the gun frantically to the left. Shannon had just been there, no more than twenty feet behind

Ferrare when he'd shot the bastard. Where was she now? He caught a glimpse of long, brunette hair obscuring a pale, grim face, but then the dark head went down. Disappeared in the crowd. Swallowed by the heaving mass of humanity.

Every ounce of control Jake had ever mastered evaporated in a flash of panic so sharp he couldn't breathe past it. Something had happened to Shannon. Lucifer Jones had her, and she was defenseless against the guy.

He'd promised he'd keep her safe from Jones.

Jake flung aside his gun, reached into his bag and grabbed a rope. Searching frantically, he sprinted for a gargoyle a few yards away, its mouth a rain downspout. He flung the end of his rope around the statue and tied it off. Without bothering to don a rappelling harness, he threw himself off the roof. The rope slid through his hands so fast it burned through the palms of his leather gloves. The pain only served to focus him on his goal. Must. Find. Shannon.

He shoved out into the panicked crowd, using all of his fighting skills to make a path to the last place he'd seen her.

Voices shouted in his earpiece. Something to the effect of what in the hell was he doing, then swearing and orders to someone to follow him. He ignored it all. His only thought was to reach Shannon. To save the woman he loved.

It took a dozen lifetimes, but finally the crowd parted for a moment and he caught a glimpse of her. She was kneeling on top of a pile of fabric, battering at it for all she was worth. Tears streamed down her cheeks, and the entire right side of her face was bloody.

Rage erupted in his gut. Someone had hurt her. And that someone would *pay*. He roared forward, his entire being demanding action.

"Shannon!" he shouted as he closed the final few yards between them.

Agonized blue eyes looked up at him, twin pools of more pain than he'd ever seen in his life.

"He won't die! You told me not to stop until he was dead, but I'm not strong enough. I can't kill him…."

Belatedly, Jake looked down at the lump she knelt on. Lucifer Jones. Beat to a pulp. Looked unconscious, too.

"I'm so sorry," she sobbed. "I. Can't. Do. It." Each word was punctuated by a blow to Lucifer's face.

His own rage broke. Gone as suddenly as it had come. He stepped forward. Dragged her to her feet and into his arms.

"I've got you, baby. You're okay. You're alive." He glanced down over the top of her head at the mess she'd made of Lucifer Jones. "And I don't think he's going to be bothering you again."

"Please finish it for me, Jake. You told me to commit to going all the way when I fight. But I'm not strong enough."

He laughed shortly. "I don't know. You're just about the strongest person I've ever met."

She shook her head in disagreement against his chest. "You'd have taken him out in two seconds."

"Doesn't look like you did too shabby, yourself. How bad did he hurt you?"

"I don't know. I just took the pain. The way you said to. I accepted the collateral damage."

Jake swore under his breath. He remembered saying the words. But he would never in a million years have guessed she'd have to apply those words for real someday. He'd give up ten years of his life for it not to be so. "I'm so sorry, Shannon. I let you down. Again."

She stared up at him blankly.

It was too late. She'd slipped away from him. He'd truly lost her. First she'd had to shoot two men, and now this. She'd all but killed a monster with her bare hands, using the very violence she most abhorred. The weight of his failure physically drove him to his knees.

"I'm...so...sorry." His words came out hoarse. Broken.

A strange wetness blossomed on his face. Everything he'd ever dreamed of—laughter, companionship, love—had been right there. His for the taking. And he'd thrown it all away because he was too wrapped up in his own guilt and self-loathing to see it. God, he'd been a fool. He stared in anguish into her eyes. "You deserve so much better than me."

Her right hand drew back and slapped him hard across the cheek. Stunned, he fell to his knees, staring at her, his face on fire.

"Jake Harrington, I wasn't kidding when I said I'd smack you if you ever said anything that stupid to me again. Don't you dare play the martyr for me. I don't want your noble self-sacrifice!"

He blinked up at her, his right eye watering profusely.

She put both of her hands on his cheeks and gazed down at him. "Jake. I forgive you. The world forgives you."

"What?"

"You can't forgive yourself for what you do. You think you're a horrible person because you kill people. But you only kill those who would hurt and kill many, many others if you didn't stop them. Take your own advice, Jake. Accept the collateral pain and push through it. Fight to live, dammit!"

"What are you talking about?" Something was starting to unfold in his heart, but he didn't have the slightest idea what it was. Maybe she could explain it. He looked up at her hopefully. Desperately.

"All these years you couldn't forgive yourself for what you do. You seem to need someone else to do it for you. So I'm doing it now. For every person you've ever killed. On behalf of your teammates, your superiors, heck, your country, I forgive you."

He stared at her a long time. Dawning understanding began to break through, but he couldn't quite believe it. Couldn't quite accept it.

"Let go of it, Jake. It's over. You've done your duty to God and country and your father and whoever else you did your job for."

It was over.

The long fight. All those years of self-denial and self-hatred. The never-ending battle to hold it all in, to pretend the pain wasn't there, to put aside the reality of what he did. The daily ritual of recalling every face of every person he'd ever killed so he'd never forget who and what he was. Over. All of it.

He wrapped his arms around Shannon's legs and buried his face against her thighs. And he cried. He finally cried. For all of them. For himself.

Shannon cried with Jake as he shook against her legs, pouring out everything he'd held inside him for who knew how long. His whole life, maybe. She laid her hands on his head in comfort and benediction and said a prayer for his soul. She didn't know what else to do.

A voice shouted in front of her, and she looked up sharply. "Howdy!" the voice called again. *Doc.*

"There you are! What in the hell are you do—" Doc broke off as Shannon made eye contact with him. He swore and then asked under the roar of the crowd around them, "You two okay?"

She laughed. She didn't have the slightest idea if they were okay or not. "Not yet. But I think maybe we will be."

"Is he hurt?" Doc gestured down at Jake.

"His hands are bleeding and look pretty torn up. And his nose looks broken."

"And you?" Doc assessed her with a medic's practiced eye.

"I've been better. But I'll live." A bolt of triumph surged through her at the realization, fueling a heady adrenaline rush. It dulled the aches and pains starting to make themselves known throughout her body.

"You two look like hell," Doc commented mildly as he slipped a rucksack off his back and started digging in it for medical supplies. He touched his throat, and Shannon heard him murmur, "We could use backup out here. Jake's in complete meltdown, but Shannon's with him. They're both mildly injured. Oh, and Shannon looks to have beat one of Ferrare's men half to death."

She looked up at the medic as he closed in to smear some cream on the side of her face.

"Are we going to be okay?" she asked him in a small voice.

"This'll numb the pain for now," Doc muttered. Then he glanced down at Jake and back up at her. "Together, I think the two of you might both make it. Love is the greatest healing force in the universe."

Gently she disentangled herself from Jake's death grip on her legs and knelt before him. He opened his eyes and looked at her like he had no idea who she was. "Come back to me, Jake. I love you."

His gaze flickered. Wonder spread across his face, once so stony and closed, but now an open book to her. She repeated the healing words, needing them almost as much as he did. "I love you."

"I love you, too," he rasped.

And that was when she knew they were going to be okay.

As long as they had love between them, there was no wound from which they couldn't heal. Together.

Tom and Tex burst out of the crowd then. The mob seemed to be dispersing as the attempted coup fell apart around them. Apparently, the deaths of the generals in charge had, indeed, taken the wind out of the rebels' sails.

Tom took one look at Lucifer on the ground behind Shannon and Jake, and his gaze narrowed. "That the guy who hurt you before?"

She nodded.

"It's your call, Shannon. A quick bullet to that bastard's head, and you'll never have to worry about him again. Lord knows he deserves it."

She frowned over at Lucifer, then looked at Jake. "What do you think?" she murmured to him.

His eyes pleaded and his lips formed the words, but no sound emerged. "No more killing."

She nodded firmly. "Jake's right. There's been enough killing."

Tom nodded, an approving glint in his eyes. "Jones is in violation of the restraining order telling him to keep away from you, and that's a parole violation. He's looking at a good long time in the slammer back in the States."

"Does Gavarone have an extradition treaty with the United States?" she asked.

Tom grinned. "It doesn't matter. President Alviedo owes us a favor. Jones is coming home with us."

She supposed Alviedo did owe them one, at that. They'd taken apart the coup attempt with an absolute minimum of bloodshed and left Alviedo firmly in control of his country.

Mac and Dutch materialized out of the thinning crowd. Mac murmured, "It was a bit dicey slipping past his bodyguards, but we confirmed the kill. Ferrare is dead. We got this off him." She looked down at the diamond ring lying in Mac's palm.

"The second ring," Tom breathed. "Sonofagun."

"Suppose there are any more doubles?" Tex drawled.

The men groaned in unison. "I doubt it," Tom replied. "Too expensive to create and too difficult to hide."

Jake shook his head and mumbled, "This was the real one. I got a long look at him and how he moves. It's over. Ferrare's dead for good."

Shannon let out a long breath. It was *all* over. Her seven-year nightmare was ended. Not only was Lucifer Jones going to be in jail for a long time to come, but she'd conquered her fear of him once and for all. And after today's beating, she suspected he wouldn't be coming looking for her again. And even if he did, Jake would be there to take care of her.

She reached out to touch Jake, running her fingertips across the planes of his face, tracing the lines on each side of his mouth and the corners of his eyes where she had big plans to install some laugh lines without delay if he'd let her.

"What happens now?" she asked him.

He frowned. "I don't know. But I know I want to do whatever comes next with you."

She laughed. "Don't even think about getting rid of me."

He gazed at her soberly. "You're my life, Shannon. My reason for living. If that's too heavy a responsibility to lay on you, I'll understa—"

She pressed her fingers to his lips. "Shh. I wouldn't have it any other way. I want to be there for you forever if you'll have me."

A hint of humor danced through his silver gaze. "Are you proposing to me?"

She blinked, startled. "I guess I am."

"Well, in that case, I guess I accept."

She stared at him in shock and murmured in disbelief, "Our grandkids are never going to believe me when I tell them I proposed to you."

And that did it. His dimples popped into view, and laugh lines crinkled at the corners of his beautiful, pain-free eyes. "Oh, they'll believe you, all right. You're a firecracker, Shannon McMahon."

"You're the whole fireworks show, Jake Harrington."

They gazed deep into each other's eyes, and all the colors of the Fourth of July unfolded inside their hearts right then and there. Yes, they were going to be just fine.

* * * * *

Don't miss Cindy Dees's next romance,
DR. COLTON'S HIGH-STAKES FIANCÉE,
the fourth in the new Silhouette Romantic Suspense
continuity miniseries
THE COLTONS OF MONTANA,
in stores September 28, 2010.

COMING NEXT MONTH

Available July 27, 2010

#1619 REDSTONE EVER AFTER
Redstone, Incorporated
Justine Davis

#1620 COVERT AGENT'S VIRGIN AFFAIR
The Coltons of Montana
Linda Conrad

#1621 ARMY OF TWO
Eagle Squadron: Countdown
Ingrid Weaver

#1622 TO CATCH A KILLER
Kimberly Van Meter

ROMANTIC SUSPENSE

REQUEST YOUR FREE BOOKS!

2 FREE NOVELS PLUS 2 FREE GIFTS!

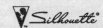

Sparked by Danger, Fueled by Passion.

YES! Please send me 2 FREE Silhouette® Romantic Suspense novels and my 2 FREE gifts (gifts are worth about $10). After receiving them, if I don't wish to receive any more books, I can return the shipping statement marked "cancel." If I don't cancel, I will receive 4 brand-new novels every month and be billed just $4.24 per book in the U.S. or $4.99 per book in Canada. That's a saving of 15% off the cover price! It's quite a bargain! Shipping and handling is just 50¢ per book.* I understand that accepting the 2 free books and gifts places me under no obligation to buy anything. I can always return a shipment and cancel at any time. Even if I never buy another book from Silhouette, the two free books and gifts are mine to keep forever.

240/340 SDN E5Q4

Name	(PLEASE PRINT)	

Address		Apt. #

City	State/Prov.	Zip/Postal Code

Signature (if under 18, a parent or guardian must sign)

Mail to the Silhouette Reader Service:

IN U.S.A.: P.O. Box 1867, Buffalo, NY 14240-1867
IN CANADA: P.O. Box 609, Fort Erie, Ontario L2A 5X3

Not valid for current subscribers to Silhouette Romantic Suspense books.

**Want to try two free books from another line?
Call 1-800-873-8635 or visit www.morefreebooks.com.**

* Terms and prices subject to change without notice. Prices do not include applicable taxes. N.Y. residents add applicable sales tax. Canadian residents will be charged applicable provincial taxes and GST. Offer not valid in Quebec. This offer is limited to one order per household. All orders subject to approval. Credit or debit balances in a customer's account(s) may be offset by any other outstanding balance owed by or to the customer. Please allow 4 to 6 weeks for delivery. Offer available while quantities last.

Your Privacy: Silhouette is committed to protecting your privacy. Our Privacy Policy is available online at www.eHarlequin.com or upon request from the Reader Service. From time to time we make our lists of customers available to reputable third parties who may have a product or service of interest to you. If you would prefer we not share your name and address, please check here. ☐

Help us get it right—We strive for accurate, respectful and relevant communications. To clarify or modify your communication preferences, visit us at www.ReaderService.com/consumerschoice.

Five hunky Texas single fathers—five stories from Cathy Gillen Thacker's LONE STAR DADS *miniseries. Here's an excerpt from the latest, THE MOMMY PROPOSAL from Harlequin American Romance.*

"I hear you work miracles," Nate Hutchinson drawled. Brooke Mitchell had just stepped into his lavishly appointed office in downtown Fort Worth, Texas.

"Sometimes, I do." Brooke smiled and took the sexy financier's hand in hers, shook it briefly.

"Good." Nate looked her straight in the eye. "Because I'm in need of a home makeover—fast. The son of an old friend is coming to live with me."

She was still tingling from the feel of his warm palm. "Temporarily or permanently?"

"If all goes according to plan, I'll adopt Landry by summer's end."

Brooke had heard the founder of Nate Hutchinson Financial Services was eligible, wealthy and generous to a fault. She hadn't known he was in the market for a family, but she supposed she shouldn't be surprised. But Brooke had figured a man as successful and handsome as Nate would want one the old-fashioned way. *Not that this was any of her business...*

"So what's the child like?" she asked crisply, trying not to think how the marine-blue of Nate's dress shirt deepened the hue of his eyes.

"I don't know." Nate took a seat behind his massive antique mahogany desk. He relaxed against the smooth leather of the chair. "I've never met him."

"Yet you've invited this kid to live with you permanently?"

"It's complicated. But I'm sure it's going to be fine."

Obviously Nate Hutchinson knew as little about teenage

boys as he did about decorating. But that wasn't her problem.
Finding a way to do the assignment without getting the least
bit emotionally involved was.

*Find out how a young boy brings Nate and Brooke
together in THE MOMMY PROPOSAL,
coming August 2010 from Harlequin American Romance.*

HAREXP0810

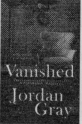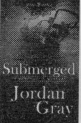